P9-CKO-068
Landon
BOOK THREE
Snow

Landon Snow

and the Island of Arcanum

R. K. MORTENSON

Other books by R. K. Mortenson

Landon Snow and the Auctor's Riddle
Landon Snow and the Shadows of Malus Quidam

ISBN 1-59789-358-7

All scripture quotations are taken from the King James Version of the Bible.

This book is a work of fiction. Names, characters, places, and incidents are either products of the author's imagination or used fictitiously. Any similarity to actual people, organizations, and/or events is purely coincidental.

Cover and interior illustrations by Cory Godbey, Portland Studios.
www.portlandstudios.com
Cover design by DogEared Design, llc.

Published by Barbour Publishing, Inc., P.O. Box 719, Uhrichsville, Ohio 44683
www.barbourbooks.com

Our mission is to publish and distribute inspirational products offering exceptional value and biblical encouragement to the masses.

Printed in the United States of America.
5 4 3 2 1

Dedication

To the men and women who serve in the

U. S. Navy

and the

U. S. Marine Corps

Fair winds and following seas

Semper Fidelis

Landon lightly gripped the pads on his thighs and tensed, awaiting the quarterback's cadence.

"Blue twenty-two, blue twenty-two. Hut. . .hut—hut-hut!"

Landon bolted forward, positioning his arms to receive the ball against his belly. As the ball struck his gut, Landon clamped his arms down, squeezing his hands over the ends of the ball. He continued moving forward, lowering his head and shoulders for the charge. The offensive line did their work and opened a hole in the defense. Landon darted up the middle, running through the lane. The goalposts came into view fifty yards away, and Landon raised his upper body for the run, cradling the football in his left arm. Sensing movement on his right flank—stomping, breathing, grabbing—Landon tucked the ball into his belly again and curled over it as he plummeted to earth.

"Oof!" he said as he struck the ground.

A body lay on top of him. Pads clicked as the tackler stood, but not before rapping Landon's helmet and taunting him.

"You're too slow, Landon Snow. I gotcha!"

Landon smiled despite himself. "Jake," he muttered to the dirt beneath his face mask. "I'll beat you next time." He knew Jake from Cornhusk Trail Elementary School, where they had been classmates. Now Landon was at Winterwild Middle School, while Jake was across town at rival Tangleriver.

Landon had made the first down, and the next play had him running the same route again. This time, he would burst through all the way for a score, he thought. If the linemen did their job and he got a good running start—

"Hut. . .hut—hut-hut!"

Landon sprang ahead and lined up his arms for the ball. As his fingers encased the points of the ball, however, a very strange thing happened. Rather than jerseys and helmets crowding in front of him, the dark shapes of several animals appeared. Five bears on their hind legs stood facing away from him, lunging and pawing, apparently trying to keep some other animals at bay. Landon stopped, frozen in his tracks. He could only watch, his heart paralyzed with fear, as a wolf leaped between two bears on the left. Then a panther came leaping around the right end. The wolf arrived first and knocked Landon flat on his back, where he lay staring at the sky. A big broad head appeared with a long muzzle and fuzzy, pointed ears.

"Icky—la boom bah!"

Landon became aware of something in his arms. *The football*, he thought with relief. At least he hadn't fumbled. Except that the football felt sort of furry. And it was panting or snuffling and seeming to curl itself up as if it were trying to burrow into his stomach. It *tickled*. Landon would have giggled if he hadn't been staring face mask to muzzle with a grinning, gloating wolf. The wolf narrowed its gleaming yellow eyes.

"Icky—la picky wicky!"

Its breathing came like the rasping of sandpaper.

"Uffa—la guffa wuffa!"

The furry creature against Landon's belly clawed at him, and Landon reflexively flung it out from beneath the wolf. The creature yelped like a rubber squeeze toy. The wolf glanced at the rolling ball of fur and rose on its hind legs. Placing its forepaws on its hips, the wolf looked down at Landon.

"Ooka-tee-*ahh*."

Landon closed his eyes. This was too weird. When he opened his eyes, Jake Adams stood with his hands on his hips, leering at Landon. Jake's big-shouldered form blocked the afternoon sun.

"What did you say?" asked Landon weakly. He was still trying to catch the wind that had been knocked out of him.

Jake leaned over, and the sun burst from behind him. Landon squinted.

"I said, 'You're too slow, Landon Snow.' And, 'I gotcha again!' "

"Oh," Landon groaned. As Jake jogged off, Landon rolled his head to his right.

A few feet away, the football rested on the grass. Landon moaned again. The referee appeared over him, stooping and scowling. His black-and-white stripes suddenly narrowed to points, and his face became long like a horse. Landon almost broke out laughing. He chomped on his mouth guard and muttered, "Zebra." Then, maybe because he felt like laughing, he said, "Hyena."

"What's that?" asked the zebra. "Are you all right?" After Landon blinked, he saw the ref again. He was waving his hand in a circular motion off to one side. "Coach! Player down here!"

Landon hardly remembered getting up or walking to the sidelines. He recalled Coach Huddle (yes, that was his name) patting his shoulder pads and asking him if he was all right and—what had happened out there? It was like he had hit a brick wall.

Not a brick wall, thought Landon. "Animals," he mumbled.

"What?" asked Coach Huddle.

"They were a bunch of animals out there, Coach," Landon explained.

As his coach frowned at him and scratched his head, Landon thought he caught a glimpse of a black-haired gorilla peering at him and flaring his nostrils. Then the gorilla—er, his coach—turned and hollered, "Strasser! Get in there for Snow! Come on, hustle, hustle!"

The rest of the game went by in a blur. Landon wasn't even sure of the final score—he was so distracted by the animals he'd seen. On the way home, the questions continued from his father.

"So," said Dad. "One minute you're charging up the middle like there's no tomorrow, and the next you're stopped cold like your feet had turned to lead. So. . . ?"

Landon knew his dad wanted an answer, but he remained quiet. He was wondering about it himself.

They slowed to a stop at a red light, and Landon's dad turned toward him. Landon stared straight ahead. Finally, his dad said, "So? What happened?"

Landon took a deep breath. The light changed, but still his

father waited. "It's green," said Landon.

His father sighed. "And it was green for you on that last run, too." He pressed the gas, and they moved forward. "No," he said, glancing at Landon. "I'm not mad, but I am curious. And concerned, of course. Your mother will probably want to know why her son was pulled from the game."

Landon always felt funny wearing his padded pants without the shoulder pads and jersey. He felt half-naked and bottom-heavy. When he looked into the mirror like this, he thought he resembled one of those mythological creatures—what were they called?—that were half man and half animal. *The bottom half goat,* Landon thought, *like a faun.* He looked like a scrawny-topped faun with thick, ungainly legs.

"I saw animals," he said. He didn't add that they were big, dark, and scary animals, other than the referee. He didn't know if he'd ever look at a referee's uniform the same again.

"Hmm," said Dad. Then with a slight smile, he added, "Well, you were playing the Tigers, you know."

Landon grimaced. "I didn't see any tigers," he said. "I mean, not like this. These animals were. . .different."

"Hmm," said his father again. They turned onto their street, passed three houses, and then eased into the fourth driveway. "You weren't on a field trip to the zoo today, were you?"

Landon groaned audibly.

"At least you didn't suffer a concussion. I was glad to hear that much." Landon's father sighed with relief as he parked the car. "The trainer said he didn't see any signs of physical trauma—other than the wind being knocked out of you." Landon's dad held the keys in midair as he turned toward Landon. "So, any other clues?

Something you ate earlier today?"

Landon shook his head. "I don't think so. It's kind of hard to explain, Dad."

His dad nodded. "All right. Well, maybe you could explain it to your mother in more detail." He raised his eyebrows.

"Maybe," said Landon. He climbed out and retrieved his pads and helmet from the backseat. *Or maybe,* he thought, approaching the door, *I'll tell Holly in more detail.* Because the truth was, he and his sister had been talking more and more about the possibilities that lay before them this weekend. And Landon wondered if he had just seen a vision that might be related somehow to the weekend's events.

What was so significant about this weekend? Landon's family was planning to visit Grandma and Grandpa Snow in Button Up, Minnesota. Which meant, of course, that Landon was hoping to sneak into the Button Up Library—the BUL—in the middle of the night, perhaps with Holly tagging along. This time, however, he would make her promise—cross her heart and hope to die—that she would not follow any slinking shadows into dark corners or down creepy stairways. At least not without Landon at her side with his trusty flashlight at the ready. Yes, Landon was anticipating another exciting midnight adventure at the end of the secret tunnel behind Grandpa Karl's bookcase. . . .

By the time Landon had put his stinky uniform away and showered and finished eating dinner, during which his father apparently decided to not even mention the "animal incident" from the football game, it was already getting dark outside. The family was eating somewhat hurriedly and quietly, the only real discussion being about who was responsible for getting the dishes loaded into the dishwasher (Holly) and how they wanted to be packed and on the road within the hour. They didn't want to arrive in Button Up too late. Otherwise, Grandma Alice was prone to worry and complain of a stomach ulcer.

"I've got to tell you something," Landon whispered to Holly as he handed her his empty plate, which she promptly slid into the rack.

"What?" She plunked in the silverware, filled the soap cup, raised the door, and clicked the switch. The machine began to whir and swish.

"Um. . . ," Landon started but then waited for his mom and dad and Bridget to leave the kitchen. They had all converged here for seemingly no reason and bumped into each other, bouncing away to different doorways like billiard balls retreating to their pockets.

"I saw animals today!" The dishwasher had dropped from a loud whirring swish to a quiet hum and swish just as Landon had spoken. "I saw *animals*," he repeated more softly. "A panther, wolf, zebra, gorilla, and bears. Lots of bears."

Holly stared at him while mindlessly wiping her hands on her sweater. "Bears," she said. "And a gorilla?" She made a face. "What do you think it means?"

Landon grinned. "That's what I want to find out." He left Holly standing there, happy in their shared confidence. What could it possibly mean? Seeing animals at a football game. . .

Time to pack for the big trip to Button Up. The sooner he was ready, the sooner they could be headed north.

As Landon stuffed his duffel bag, his mind replayed the weird images from the football game. Landon paused, holding a pair of rolled-up socks, as he remembered the bundle of fur he'd been "holding" when the wolf tackled him. It wasn't a cat; he was quite sure. It had seemed rather light and springy, though. Was it some sort of rodent, perhaps? A rabbit or a squirrel? *No, it was different from those, too.* Landon smiled and shook his head as he noticed the socks in his hand. He threw them into the bag. *It was a* football, *you dummy.*

"Two-minute warning!"

Landon jumped. His mother had just disappeared from his doorway when she popped back in again. "By the way, how did your game go? Did you win?"

"It went okay," said Landon.

His mother raised her eyebrows as if to say, "And. . . ?"

"I've got to finish packing," said Landon evasively.

"That's right. We gotta get on the road, Snows." Her voice trailed down the hallway. "Let's load up!"

Landon forced himself to concentrate. Did he have everything he'd need for the weekend trip? He rifled through his clothing and found the plastic case of his flashlight, heavy with fresh batteries. What else did he need? Oh yes, one more item. Closing his old, worn leather Bible, Landon lifted it from the desk and nestled it among his clothes inside his duffel bag. All he wondered now was which pages the Bible would turn to in Grandpa Karl's study. For he knew that the underlined words he found on those pages would determine the course of his next adventure.

By the time Landon, Holly, Bridget, and their parents reached Grandma and Grandpa Snow's house in Button Up, it was late and dark. With their tummies full from their quick dinner, even Landon and Holly didn't stand a chance of staying awake for three hours in the car. As usual, Bridget had fallen asleep within ten minutes of leaving the driveway. When their father opened his door and let in a wave of chill air, Bridget bristled.

"What? What happened? Where am I?"

Landon smiled to himself. A trip just wasn't complete without Bridget's disoriented questions upon arrival. "Get out of the ca–ah–ahhhr, Bridget," said Landon, breaking into a yawn. "We're he–ee–eere."

Landon couldn't believe how tired he was. Even Grandma Alice's delicious lemon bars—of which he ate two—washed down with milk for a bedtime treat didn't wake him up. He only felt more tired. He and Holly eyed each other lazily across the table. Then she went upstairs without a word to him, offering only a halfhearted "good night" to everyone. Bridget had already gone up to bed and was assuredly out like a light.

With one creak toward the top, Holly's steps receded up the stairs. The house fell quiet save for the soft *tick-tock* from the clock in the hall. "Well," Grandpa Karl said finally. "I suppose it's too late for a story tonight." He cocked an eyebrow at Landon as if this were a question. Landon could only slowly shake his head.

"I'm tired, Grandpa. Maybe—ahh-ahhh*hhh*—excuse me. Tomorrow night?"

Grandpa Karl's eyes lit up. He tugged at his gray beard thoughtfully. "Tomorrow night," he said.

After saying thanks and good night, Landon shuffled to the study. He barely had the strength to brush his teeth and change into his pajamas. Thankfully, the sleeping bag had been laid out on the sofa for him, and he climbed willingly into it. One small part of him said he should check his Bible for mysteriously turning pages before he fell asleep, but that small part was quickly snuffed out by darkness and dreams.

The next day, Landon awoke feeling refreshed until he remembered the previous night and how easily he had gone to sleep. *Oh no!* He worried he might have missed his opportunity for an adventure. Unzipping the sleeping bag and quickly climbing out, he stepped across the cold floor to the desk. The Bible was there, and it was closed. Landon ran his finger along the roughened edge of the great book and sighed. *I'm sorry I fell asleep,* he prayed, although he wasn't sure if he was apologizing to God or to himself. *If there's something else I'm supposed to see—a vision or a dream—and something I'm supposed to do, well, I hope that it still happens.* Landon opened his eyes and looked up. Then he closed his eyes again in a long blink. *Soon.* Opening his eyes, he said aloud, "Amen." Then he shivered.

The draft he felt only came from beneath the door to the hallway. Otherwise the air—and everything else in the room—was still. Landon flopped the Bible open and let the pages fall where they may. The two pages facing him were in the book of Leviticus. Landon leaned closer, his heart galloping—but only for a moment. Not a single sentence had been underlined on either page. He took a deep breath and sighed forcefully, pretending he wasn't trying to turn the pages with his breath when really he was. By the time the page began to quiver, Landon thought he was about to faint. He quit blowing and walked to the bookcase. Again pretending to look away, he tried to nudge the bookcase. It wouldn't budge. Exasperated, Landon let his whole body shiver, and then he put on his clothes and left the study for breakfast.

"Aren't my pancakes as good as usual?" Grandma Alice asked, pausing to study Landon as she set another plate on the table, stacked and steaming.

"What?" Landon looked up. He'd been poking at his pancake with his fork. "Oh, they're good, Grandma. I'm just not as hungry as usual." He thought about saying more, but there wasn't much else to say.

Holly caught his eye from across the table. She raised her eyebrows and half tilted her head as if to say, "Well. . . ?"

Landon knew she was wondering if anything had happened last night. This was all he needed, for his sister to rub it in. He lowered his head and gave a stealthy half shake. He had soaked up the excess syrup on his plate with the one piece of pancake he'd been sliding around. He put the piece into his mouth and made himself swallow.

"Are you tired, Landon?" It was his mom.

"No, not really."

"Still sore about the football ga—"

Landon frowned at his dad, and his dad changed direction in midsentence.

"I mean, you took a pretty good hit or two from—what's his name again? That boy you went to school with last year."

"Jake," said Landon, sighing. "Jake Adams. Yeah, he tackled me, but I'm not too sore." *Not about that anyway,* Landon thought. He was sore because this weekend would turn out to be a big waste of time if he didn't get to go through the tunnel behind Grandpa Karl's bookcase.

"Grandpa?" asked Holly. Something in her voice made Landon look at her. "Are there many animals around here? I mean, do you and Grandma ever see strange wildlife?" Landon thought he detected a slight smirk pinching the corner of her mouth. He glared at her, but her gaze was fixed on Grandpa Karl.

"Ohhh yeah!" said Bridget, perking up. "Can we see some animals?" She looked eagerly at Grandpa Karl and then at Mom and Dad as if she might need permission from them to see some animals.

"Well," Grandpa Karl said after taking a sip of coffee, "we do see a fair amount of deer this time of year. And of course there are the birds. . .at the feeder, and the squirrels. . .at the feeder. And raccoons—"

"Deer," said Grandma Alice, who was finally sitting down to serve herself a pancake.

"I said deer already," said Grandpa Karl.

"Oh. And cats," said Grandma Alice. She smiled at Bridget. "You know about the cats."

Grandpa Karl muttered something under his breath.

"They live in the shed," said Grandma Alice. "Your grandfather loves the cats."

Grandpa Karl mumbled something else. Then he said, "At least they catch the mice. Otherwise they'd be living there, too."

"We had another litter last spring," said Grandma Alice. "And most of the kittens have decided to stay on this time."

Grandpa Karl blew over his coffee, although Landon was sure it was no longer too hot. "She won't let me get rid of the cats," said Grandpa Karl quietly.

"He really does love them." Grandma Alice beamed at Grandpa Karl as he stared off into space. But then he smiled, and she resumed eating her pancake.

"Anything else?" said Holly, persisting. What was she driving at? Landon wondered. "Do you ever see any other animals? Like bears?"

Landon choked even though no food was in his mouth. He stood abruptly, leaving half a pancake on his plate and nearly upsetting the whole table. "Excuse me," he said. "The pancake's good, Grandma. Maybe I'll finish it later."

"Where are you off to all of a sudden, Landon?" asked his mom.

Landon hesitated, unsure of what to say. What he *wanted* to say was, "I'm getting away from Holly right after I punch her." And he *wanted* to lean across the table and do just that. Mercifully, his grandfather interceded with a suggestion.

"Perhaps you'd like to take a walk. . .down to the library?"

Landon turned, thinking he didn't feel like taking a walk down there or anywhere at the moment. He only wanted to go and sulk alone in his room. Or in Grandpa Karl's study, anyway.

"It looks like a nice day for it," Grandpa Karl added. "And oh yes, lots of Canada geese flying through in big Vs," he said, nodding to Bridget. Then to Holly he said, "Other animals, but no bears, I'm afraid." Grandpa Karl looked at Landon and winked. Landon wasn't sure why, but something about his grandfather's wink made his heart skip a beat. He thought of Hardy, his big goofy grin and those sudden winks, which always seemed to catch Landon off guard. *He knows something.* That's what Landon thought after seeing Hardy wink. *He knows more than he's letting on.* But could this be true of his grandfather, as well? Or had his wink merely been a twitch of his muscles?

Could it be chance, mere circumstance. . . ?

"All right," said Landon. "That's a good idea. I think I'll go for a walk." As soon as he said it, the idea sounded like a good one, indeed. His heart began to rise with anticipation as he turned to go get his shoes.

"Why don't the girls go with you?" suggested his dad.

Landon froze, his heart sinking fast. He was about to step away, pretending he hadn't heard, when his mother chimed in. "That's a great idea, honey. The fresh air will do you all good. Such a beautiful day outside!"

Landon was tempted to reply with sarcasm, "Then why don't you and Dad go out and enjoy it?" But he knew that answer would do him no good. Instead, he swallowed hard and stalked off. Entering the hallway, he turned back and shouted, "Five minutes!" To which he heard Bridget's high-pitched reply: "Yippee! Canada geese and the library!"

Landon stomped into the study, though his stockinged feet stung more than they made noise. It took everything in him to keep from slamming the door. He sat on the sofa and dropped his head into his hands. This trip was not going at all as he had planned! *Argh!* If there was one animal he wanted to see, it was a big dark horse named Melech. *Melech,* he thought tenderly. Suddenly he wanted to cry.

Slipping on his canvas sneakers, Landon stormed from the room and strode toward the front entry. "Five minutes are up!" he shouted.

A chair scraped in the dining room. "That woven't five minutes!" Holly cried, with her mouth apparently full of pancake.

"Well, I'm going for a walk now." Landon had his hand on the door, but something kept him from opening it. What was it? A funny thought occurred to him. "Holly?" he called over his shoulder.

She was hopping out from the dining room, struggling to get a shoe on. She was also still chewing. "Fwhat?"

"Do you have your backpack here?" He turned just enough to see her. She was nodding, hopping.

"Uh-huh." Swallow. "Why?"

"Go get it," he said without explanation. "You're bringing it."

She paused, and Landon sensed the tension in the air. He waited, watching from the corner of his eye. Finally, Holly dropped the shoe she'd been working on and went up the stairs, her one shoe clomping and her other foot, shoeless, falling softly on the steps. When Holly came back down with her backpack, Bridget also emerged, ready to go. Holly sat down quietly to put on her other shoe. When she stood, she and Bridget looked expectantly at their brother. Landon stared back at them. Without a word, he returned to the study, retrieved his Bible, and came back out. Then he opened the door and stepped outside.

"We don't even need jackets; it's so nice." Holly was carrying her backpack by one of its straps in one hand, swinging it back and forth. "It's like one more day of summer sneaking in before winter comes. That's ninety-two and a quarter."

The gravel on the long driveway crunched beneath their shoes. "It's not *that* hot," said Landon. "Not even close. Maybe seventy-two, if even."

Holly giggled. "Not *degrees*, Landon. *Days*. With an extra day of summer, that'd be ninety-two. And a quarter. That's 365 divided by—"

"All right, all right. I get it." Landon sped up to be a few paces ahead of them. He stopped abruptly and spun on his heel. "Here," he said thrusting the Bible toward Holly. "You're carrying this. That's why you brought your backpack."

Holly skidded to a halt. Her blond hair shone in the sun. "Why are you so mad at me?" She flared her eyes when she said "mad." "I didn't do anything."

Bridget looked back and forth between her older siblings. "Is it the pancake, Landon? You only ate half."

"Yeah," said Holly nodding. "You usually eat three or four, even five during football season."

Landon stood proudly at the mention of his eating capacity. He *was* growing taller. And after these twelve long years, he was finally—*finally*—stretching noticeably farther up than Holly. Well, it wasn't quite twelve full years *yet*. His birthday was tomorrow. Too bad he couldn't pull away from being only 341 days older than Holly. At least they didn't look so much like twins anymore.

Landon glanced at Bridget before addressing Holly. "Why did you have to talk about the animals? Huh? I trusted you not to tell anyone." Landon made a snorting *humph* sound for emphasis.

Bridget's eyes grew wider, and she tilted back her head of dark curls. "What about them?" she said. "What about the animals?" She lowered her head and turned this way and that, bouncing her curls. "Where are they? Oh!" She pointed and then slowly drew her finger up in a straight line toward the sky. Landon heard them before he saw them. A big V of geese soon passed overhead, raucously honking.

"It's lopsided," he said absentmindedly.

"Eight on one side and seven on the—"

"Stop," said Landon. "Just stop. Don't say anything. And carry this." He handed Holly his Bible, and she quietly took it and stuffed it into her backpack, though her lips were pushed out in a pout. Landon turned and resumed marching, hearing tiny pebbles grinding behind him from his sisters' footsteps. The grating noise quieted when they reached the road and wound their way down the hill among the half-barren trees.

The sight of the Button Up Library always inspired Landon, and this morning was no exception. He could see it from behind through the trees as they reached the bottom of the hill, and his heart swelled as the tall columns came into view around front.

Amazingly, Holly kept quiet as they climbed the steps—*all forty-two of them*, Landon couldn't help thinking. Even more amazing was what they found at the top of the steps. The library, which was not scheduled to open for another hour and a half, had an unlocked door.

Even Bridget's little voice echoed in the tall marble lobby. "Do you think we should be in here?"

Landon's shoes squeaked as if he were on a basketball court. He finally resorted to walking on his tiptoes to keep them quiet. The chandelier sparkled high overhead. As they passed by the rowboat-shaped tombstone for the library's famous founder, Bartholomew G. Benneford, Landon stopped, *squeak*, and motioned for his sisters to stop too.

"Listen," he said, half turning his head. "What is that noise?"

It sounded rather like a drum. Like one of those big drums in a symphony orchestra—a kettle drum or timpani. *Plumb. Plumb.*

It was quiet.

And then—*plumb*.

"Over there," said Bridget, her voice light as a feather.

At the far end of the lobby, opposite the log wall of Bart's Reading Room, something round and large and red sat on the floor. *Plumb.* Bridget was right; the sound seemed to be coming from it. They crept closer, and a tiny swift movement caught Landon's eye. Just before it fell into the big red tub—for that was what was on the floor—Landon realized what it was: *a drop of water—*

Plumb!

The red tub was almost big enough to be a child's wading pool. It was about half full of water, catching drips from the ceiling. Holly reached out her hand to catch the next one—*split*—and then she wiped it on her pants. "If I had been here when the leak started, I could tell you how many droplets are in the tub."

"It looks like millions to me," said Bridget, gazing into the pool.

"Hmm." Holly leaned over, scrutinizing the depth and width as if she could actually determine the volume in drops.

Landon was staring toward the ceiling. "I wonder how long it's been leaking and how come they haven't fixed it yet."

Plumb.

With the mystery of the drum sound solved, the Snow children soon turned their attention to the rest of the library. It was clearly vacant; perhaps someone had failed to lock the door the previous night. Having the place to themselves was rather pleasant. Not that it was ever overly crowded, vast library that it was, and in such a tiny town. Landon wandered down the hallway toward the main collection room, checking back to see Holly and Bridget entering Bart's Reading Room across the way. At the end of the corridor, Landon turned left, feeling his heart crawling into his throat as he approached the corner. The carpeting muted his footsteps, and he crept quietly as a cat.

"Hello," he said to the giant wall of books. "I'm back again. It's me."

After a pause, Landon tried his greeting again. Nothing. "So you're not too talkative today, huh?" His heart was hammering as he gently tapped a few of the books' spines with his fingertips. The anticipation was killing him. He just needed one book to talk, to clear its throat or make a sound—something to break the silence and get it over with.

"Why aren't you—?" Landon started, but then he stopped. *Of course,* he thought somewhat sadly. *It's daytime.* He had never heard the books talk in the daytime. *You only come out at night, right?* With a sigh, he turned and walked away, heading for the center of the room.

The *Book of Meanings* held its place of pride amid the stacks in the reference section. All alone atop its stand. So big and broad and yet so. . .ordinary. Landon flipped a page and glanced at the boldface word above his finger. *Island: noun, a solitary body of land entirely surrounded by water.* Landon sighed. It was just a big book. He paused and tilted his head. He thought he'd heard the timpani sound.

His next stop was at the base of the metal stairway called "the tree." The floor was completely carpeted around it. No grate, no sign saying KEEP OUT or COME IN, no hole with steps spiraling down into the earth. Only a worn patch of carpet over a quite solid floor.

"Hey."

Landon gasped, spinning on his heel.

"Holly! Don't sneak up on me like that!"

"I wasn't sneaking. So," she said, studying the floor, "it's gone, huh?"

"Yeah," said Landon, tamping the spot for effect. "Boy, this place is so normal during the day. It's almost freaky."

Holly grinned when Landon looked at her, and he laughed. "Yeah," she said. "No talking books or secret passageways—"

"You checked behind the bookcase?"

Holly nodded. "Bart's books look like they haven't been moved in years."

"It's just plain weird," said Landon, smiling.

"Totally."

"Hey. Where is Bridget?"

"Oh. She's still back in the reading room. I kind of wanted to come in here first, you know?"

Landon nodded.

"And," said Holly, "I figured you'd want to come in here by yourself first."

Landon looked up at the tree's metal walkways shooting in every direction at various heights. "Thanks," he said. "And I'm sorry for being mad before."

"Me, too. I mean, about the animals."

"Yeah, well. . .I'd almost forgotten about them already." Landon looked back toward the lobby. "That was weird yesterday at the game. I'm not sure what that was all about. Bears."

"And a panther and a wolf and—"

"All right, all right. Don't push it, Holly. We'd better go get Bridget. I'm actually a little hungry."

"And we should leave before somebody comes and catches us."

"Aw, what are they going to do, blame us for the leak?"

Landon gave Holly a playful shove. Then he took hold of her shoulder and spun her around. "Where's your backpack?"

"I left it with Bridget in the cabin. She wasn't interested in any of Bart's old books, so I said she could look at your Bible."

"Which of course *is* one of his old books," said Landon. "But I don't like other people looking at it." He gave his sister a stern look.

Holly shrugged. "What was I supposed to do? *You* gave it to me, Landon."

Landon shook his head and brushed past her. As he neared the corridor, he could hear the water dripping again. The sound was lighter and steadier than before. Halfway across the lobby, he paused, issuing a half-court squeak, and decided to go look into the tub. To his amazement, it was nearly three-quarters full. And the water was coming down in an almost steady stream.

"Hol–ly!" His rising voice echoed loudly. "Come look at this!"

Holly looked up and down at the falling water and then at Landon. "Is it raining outside?"

He hadn't even thought of that. The faraway glass doors glowed brightly with sunlight. "Doesn't look like it. It was beautiful out, remember?"

"But where's this water coming from? Is there plumbing up there?"

"There must be," said Landon. Just then, they both jumped at the sound of something like a pipe bursting after a loud groaning, wrenching noise. Landon and Holly stared at one another, wide-eyed.

"Landon?" It was Bridget. Something in her voice caused

Landon to ignore the rushing *ssshhh* sound that had started in the walls. "Landon?" Bridget was standing in the doorway to the reading room, but she wasn't looking at Landon and Holly. She was staring at something in her hands.

"What is it, Bridget? Are you okay?" Landon felt Holly's hand on his arm as they went over to their little sister. Landon hardly noticed that, instead of squeaking, his shoes were now making soft splashing sounds along the floor.

"Landon. . .look at this. . .look. . ." Bridget still hadn't looked up from what she was holding. It was a book. Landon's Bible.

"What's wrong, Bridge—"

Landon and Holly stopped simultaneously. All three children stared at the Bible and watched as pages rose from one side and fell to the other. Landon reached down and gently took the Bible from Bridget, noticing her trembling hands. He held the Bible down low so Bridget could watch as the final pages fluttered up and over. When the last page had settled and Landon had his wits gathered about him, he looked at the text.

"It's in Genesis," he said. "Chapter seven. And some verses are underlined." He was vaguely aware that something strange was going on in the lobby, but at the moment, he was too excited about reading the underlined verses to care. His own hands had begun to quiver. "Here," he said, raising the Bible to better see it. "Verse eleven: 'In the six hundredth year of Noah's life, in the second month, the seventeenth day of the month, the same day were all the fountains of the great deep broken up, and the windows of heaven were opened.' And verse twelve: 'And the rain was upon the earth forty days and forty nights.' "

At that point, Landon had to quit reading. A loud gushing noise filled the room, and the children suddenly noticed that their feet were soaked. The leak from the corner had become a waterfall, overflowing the red tub and somehow spilling enough water onto the floor to a level almost halfway up the *outside* of the tub. The children stood transfixed for several seconds, gazing in wonder at the chamber that was rapidly becoming an aquarium.

"Landon."

He hardly heard Holly's voice over the roar.

"Landon!"

Holly's shout still sounded soft and faraway, even though she was practically screaming into his ear.

"What! I can't hear you!"

"What do we do?"

This was a very good question, considering the water was climbing up around his knees.

"We'd better run for it! The door!"

Holly nodded, and they both grabbed one of Bridget's arms. She was whimpering, Landon thought, judging by her face. But he couldn't hear it.

Running proved impossible. They could only wade and slosh and then slog their way through, hoisting Bridget ever higher over the water.

"It's too much!" said Landon, struggling to keep both Bridget's face and his Bible dry. The water had reached his ribs and was sloshing just below Holly's armpits. If they'd had their swimsuits on instead of their clothes, they could have just swum to the door. But by the time they reached it, the door would be underwater, and Landon wasn't sure Bridget could hold her breath for the dive.

And why was he thinking like this anyway? Of course they hadn't brought their swimsuits! They were going for a walk to the library, for crying out loud. Landon had to think fast. Holly was beginning to gasp, and Bridget was sputtering. Above him—could it be?—a tinkling sound was heard amid the whooshing echoes. The chandelier. It sounded like a beckoning wind chime. Landon turned to look not at it but at what was beneath it.

Bartholomew G. Benneford's rowboat tombstone.

For one long second, Landon looked at it, wondering. The thing wasn't a real boat. It was made of *stone.* But shouldn't it be underwater by now? How was it still. . .afloat?

"Lan—!" Holly's voice was cut short by a glubbing sound. There wasn't time.

Landon leaned and got his arm around Bridget beneath her armpits. But the water had begun to undulate in waves. He couldn't do this, not with one hand. In one heart-wrenching moment, he made the decision, and he let his Bible go.

"Come on," Landon said, urging himself. He grabbed Bridget and carried her to the boat. Hoisting her up so she could clamber on board, for one terrifying moment, Landon felt his feet leave the floor as the water swelled. He came back down and turned around. "Holly!"

Holly had been carried another foot away by the wave. Thrashing her way toward Landon, she finally came within reach, and Landon grabbed her hands and pulled her toward him. Then he helped her up and into the boat. Where was his

Bible? There. It was still floating somehow, rising and falling with the water. Landon was tempted to swim for it. But then it fluttered a few pages as if waving good-bye and sank behind the next swell.

Landon felt a stab in his chest, and his face tightened with pain. "No!" A mouthful of water convinced him to turn around, grab hold of the boat, and climb on board.

It didn't seem possible that the waterfall, torrential as it was, could fill up the library like this. *There must be leaks in the floor or the walls, too*, Landon thought. It was too noisy to try to communicate anything out loud.

It also didn't seem possible that the stone rowboat was afloat. Didn't stone sink? And this tombstone was made of solid marble. Yet here it was, rising with the ascent of water.

That's when Landon noticed that the stone had turned to wood. The oars, which had always been wood, were now clicking back and forth in their brass oarlocks. Thank goodness they hadn't fallen out and floated away. Then again, what good would oars do them inside a library?

Holly held Bridget, who appeared to be shivering from cold or fear or both. Now that they had made it into the boat, they couldn't do much else but wait to see what happened next. Would the water continue to rise all the way to the ceiling? *Then* what would they do? Landon thought he'd better start trying to think of something. He didn't want his sisters and him to get trapped inside the boat at the top. He also didn't want them to drown. But what could they do?

Apparently, the flood had affected the whole library, as other books came floating in from the main collection room.

Then Landon noticed something else peculiar. The stone book propped in the prow of Bart's tombstone had become a real book, complete with paper pages that were flapping and turning. The rowboat swiveled this way and that, pivoting, as if it were getting anxious for something.

Another twenty feet higher and they would crash into the chandelier. Then Holly could really, finally count the crystals for herself. She'd always wanted to do that. This thought didn't encourage Landon much, however. And he doubted it would comfort Holly at this point, either.

They continued to swivel like an upright washing-machine rotor. They also continued to rise.

Fifteen feet to the chandelier.

Ten.

Five.

The waterfall was shrinking against the rising water level and growing quieter. Though the chandelier was nearly on top of them, it itself hung perhaps ten feet below the ceiling. Why were they still directly beneath it? With a flash of inspiration—and a mental kick for not thinking of this earlier—Landon sat on the bench behind his sisters and took hold of the oars. He stroked with all his might, propelling water away from the boat in small waves. Still the boat remained fix in its position.

Tensing, Landon looked up, prepared to call for everyone to abandon ship. The tinkling crystals of the chandelier were close. They were extremely close. Landon could almost reach up and touch them. But they didn't seem to be getting any closer. After waiting several seconds, still ready to issue the command for evacuation, Landon almost felt like laughing, he was so relieved. They had stopped! Barely out of reach of the chandelier.

Then the waterfall itself ceased. It slowed to a trickle and then a final few drops. The only remaining noise came from water sloshing along the sides of the boat and gently slapping at the walls.

"Are you okay?" Landon asked. "Holly? Bridget?" His voice echoed like the lifeguard's at the middle school pool.

His sisters were staring like zombies, their eyes and mouths open wide. Poor Bridget's usually curly hair drooped in long, sad spirals. She looked like a scared, wet puppy.

Landon stood and took them both in his arms. One of them shuddered and set them all shivering. They stood together like that awhile, the three of them, trembling. Landon glanced up at the chandelier, just to be sure, and thought of mentioning to Holly that here was her chance to count the crystals. But Holly spoke first.

"Hey," she said, flinching at the loudness of her own voice. Lowering her tone, she tried again. "Hey, look over there. My backpack!"

"And l–l–l–o–o–o–k over th–th–there," said Bridget. She worked her arm free and pointed. "A f–f–fish!"

"What?" Landon was trying to determine if the puffy, brown-looking object was indeed Holly's backpack, when Bridget's statement swerved his attention. "A fish, Bridget? Are you sure?" What on earth would a fish be doing in the library?

"Oh," said Landon, spotting it. Indeed it was a fish floating on its side, its head and tail curled inwardly away from the surface of the water.

"That is one old, dead fish," said Holly. And just as she said it, the fish tipped over and sank.

A gentle swell had Landon and his sisters grabbing the boat's sides and each other for balance. None of them seemed ready to sit again, however.

"I g–g–guess it's going back to Bart's Re–Re–Reading Room." Bridget lowered her arm and snuggled against her big brother. "I'm s–s–sorry, Landon." She closed her eyes, and Landon felt a drop of water hit his hand. Was Bridget crying? A sudden shudder accompanied by a sob gave him his answer.

He hugged her tighter. "Oh, Bridget. It's okay. It's not your fault. We'll, uh, we'll figure something out. Won't we, Holly?" Maybe Holly could come up with some sort of a mathematical solution to their problem.

"No," said Bridget. "I had your B–B–Bible. And now it's gone. And now th–th–this! I've ruined the whole li–li–library!"

Landon sighed. He was sad about losing his Bible. He hadn't even considered the rest of the books in the library—or the damage to the historical landmark itself. His stomach began to turn, although he was not about to blame Bridget for any of this. Their biggest problem remained being in a seemingly immovable boat atop a lot of water in the lobby of a library.

Holly had removed herself from their small huddle and was trying out the oars. Water splashed, and the boat turned, but it would not go forward or backward. Neither would it allow itself to be turned all the way around. It would go only so far before springing back to its original position. Landon and Bridget swiveled like dancers on a music box, swaying against the boat's pivots.

"It's almost like it's anchored or something," said Holly, as if making a merely casual observation.

"That's it!" said Landon, suddenly growing excited. He wasn't sure why he was getting excited, other than that Holly had surely figured out the reason why the boat had remained fixed in its position. And this new information gave him something he could begin trying to figure out: how to use this new knowledge of an anchor—and logically, a chain—to figure out a way to get them back to the floor and eventually out the front door of the library.

The boat swiveled to the right, and then it swung back round to the left, only to straighten out again.

"Quit doing that, Holly. We're anchored. I'm trying to think."

"And I'm getting woozy," complained Bridget. "I'm sitting down."

"I'm *not* doing it," said Holly. "I'm not touching the oars!"

Exasperated, Landon closed his eyes and sighed. This was *not* the time for playing games. Holly should know better—

"Hey, everybody," said Bridget. Her stutter was gone and her voice rose in pitch. "Look!"

"We know about the fish," said Landon harshly. "There are more important things to consider—"

The boat abruptly swiveled, and Landon nearly tumbled overboard.

"Holly!" he shouted with a half turn. Except Holly was no longer sitting on the bench.

And neither was Bridget.

They were standing together in the front of the boat, staring at the open book in the prow.

"Landon. . ." Holly's voice sounded strangely tense. "You'd better come look at this."

Landon joined his sisters, swaying together as the boat pitched them leisurely back and forth. Except it wasn't only the boat that was moving on its own. The pages in the book were turning, as well.

Landon's throat felt dry and pinched. "What on earth?" was all he could manage to say. The turning of the pages and the turning of the boat were connected. As a sheaf of pages rose and then fell to the right, the boat swerved in that direction. And when the pages flipped to the left, the boat immediately followed suit.

Landon wanted to say, *What on earth?* again, but he could only watch breathlessly as the book's pages flew to the left and to the right, magically maneuvering the boat beneath them.

A large clump of pages stopped abruptly in midair, hovered a moment as the boat became still, and then split apart to either side of the book. The boat remained calm, aligned, it seemed, to its original orientation. The book appeared perfectly balanced, opened once again to where it had begun, right in the middle. The crazy, dizzying boat ride was apparently over.

Landon was just about to let himself relax when he noticed the words on the pages of the book.

Had the words been there before? Or had they only just appeared? One word was printed on each page. The left page said, "ANCHOR," and the right page said, "AWEIGH."

" 'Anchor aweigh'?" said Landon.

A metallic clink sounded faintly from the depths below.

Holly whispered, "Did you hear that?"

No one had time to respond, however. The next instant saw the water before them dropping away as the water behind them grew into a giant swell, pitching them headlong into the abyss.

Hold on!" Landon yelled over his sisters' screams. They were already holding on. Landon had grabbed the right side of the book and was hugging Bridget with his left arm. Holly had done the same on the other side, using her opposite arm around Bridget. Meanwhile, Bridget had no choice but to hold the bottom edge of the book in which her face was nearly planted.

The water fell away before them, but not entirely. Indeed, it now appeared to be rising back toward them as they plummeted downward. "Hold—" Landon started to shout again, but the abrupt impact cut him off.

What he'd wanted to say this time, though, was, "Hold your breath!" For he was fully expecting them to be submerged and have to fight their way back up for air. And then, in that split second when one's life—or in this case, one's death—flashes before one's eyes, Landon thought he'd also better soon shout, "Let go!" if they were not to go down with the boat.

Instead of a mouthful of water, however, what Landon

got was the wind knocked out of him. After being thrust bolt upright, he found himself grasping for dear life to keep from falling backward. This was worse than the world's swiftest roller coaster—or, perhaps it was better, if only he had been prepared for what was coming.

"Whoa!" said Holly. Bridget soon followed with a resounding, "Wow!" All before Landon had gathered his wits enough to say, "Are you all right? Are we all. . .all right?" Then he joined his sisters' gazes and stared straight ahead. His own mouth dropped open, and he heard himself say, "Whaaa. . .whaaa. . .whaaat is this?"

Looking down, he saw no water. But a floor, or a deck rather, of wooden planks stretched away before them. Rising from the deck was a tall telephone pole—no, a mast—with other poles or limbs extending from it horizontally. And from these limbs hung giant sheets that were billowing out away from them like parachutes. "Sails," Landon muttered under his breath. "Those are sails."

Something welled up inside him, and before he knew what he was doing, Landon shouted, "Hoist the mainsail! Lower the jib!"

The ship rocked forward, groaning. Then it rose back up, creaking.

Noticing his sisters staring at him, Landon grinned. "A kid at school says that all the time. I have no idea what a jib is."

Holly and Bridget glanced at each other and shrugged. Then all three of them looked forward and crowed together, "Hoist the mainsail! Lower the jib!"

As if in response, the huge sails rippled and fluttered before snapping full out.

Speaking of crowing, the only thing visible above the barricade of sailcloth was what Landon guessed to be the crow's nest. The cuplike fixture sat high atop another tall mast, topped by a rippling white pennant. Beyond the crow's nest, the sky appeared to teeter back and forth. A tapered rope web ran up to the crow's nest. In fact, there were ropes going up everywhere on the ship. Single ropes, double ropes, and webs connecting the railing on either side to the masts. A vision of circus performers—climbing, swinging, and balancing on the beams—danced momentarily before Landon's eyes.

Though the forward view was all ship, the view to either side and behind them was nearly all water. Landon had never seen the sea before, let alone sailed on it. The sight took his breath away.

"There's no steering wheel," Bridget said matter-of-factly.

"What?"

Landon looked at his hands. For some reason, he'd thought he'd been holding two prongs or spokes of the steering wheel. What was a ship's wheel called? A *helm*. What he was actually holding were the edges of the book.

"What?" he repeated in dismay. The appearance of the ship had practically erased the memory of Bart's rowboat, including its book, from his mind.

"How will we steer?" said Holly. "The oars are gone, too. Well, except for those."

By *those,* Holly meant narrow walkways that extended from where they were standing out over the water on either side of the ship. The walkways ended in circles or little platforms so that they looked like enlarged, flattened oars. Sort of. The walkways were railed in by two ropes.

"Well," said Landon, referring to the steering problem, "that's a good question. The helm should be right here"—he patted the book and felt proud for using the word *helm*—"shouldn't it? But instead, it looks like everything's changed *except* the book." In a fit of disgust, Landon heaved the front cover, closing the book.

The ship lurched so hard to the right that Landon found himself crushing his sisters against the rail. Thankfully, they'd missed the walkway, or they could have found themselves rushing right into—or over—the ropes. Here the railing was wood.

"Oof!"

"Ow. I can't breathe."

Landon looked back at the book. *Could it really—*

Before he finished his thought, he lunged, fighting gravity to make it to the book. With all his strength, he pried it open and turned back the pages in stacks. When it was open near the middle again, the ship righted and sailed fairly smoothly and steadily on. Landon's knees wobbled after the fact, and he collapsed to the deck.

"What are you trying to do, sink us?" Holly was looking a little shaky herself. She tried to hide it by brushing herself off, even though there was nothing there.

Bridget took a step from the rail, waited for the ship's gentle dip and rise, and then took another wary step. "I don't think"—she stretched her arms for balance—"we should ever close the book." She reached the solid railing that ran along either side of the book and held on.

Keeping one hand on each side of the book, Landon slowly stood. His knees were still shaking. Who would have guessed a single book could move the whole world?

"Good idea, Bridge." Landon grinned at her. "Get it? This is the bridge, right?" He tapped his foot on the deck.

"First Mate Holly, please report to the bridge." Landon spoke in his most captainlike voice.

"Landon?"

Bridget was looking up at him. Her limp hair was beginning to tighten back into curls. Her brown eyes were as large as a puppy's.

"Yeah, Bridge. What is it?"

"I'm sorry we lost your Bible."

Something tugged at the back of Landon's throat. He forced a swallow. "*Ahem*. Well, who knows? Maybe we'll find it again someday." He had to look away from her, so he stared at the sails.

"It might be a little hard to find anything out here," said Holly. "Look at all that water. How many drops do you think—"

Landon glared at her. Holly's thirst for such unknowable knowledge had led her down a dark path before, when she was enticed by Malus Quidam's shadows. Malus Quidam was the evil one who sought to destroy the good created by the Auctor. Landon discovered the Auctor was Author and Creator of all when he solved the Auctor's Riddle.

"Uh," said Holly reacting to her brother's stare. "Well, there's a lot, anyway. A trillion cubed at least. . ."

"Holly!" But when Landon looked again, she was grinning. He smiled back at her. "Yeah, there is a lot of water."

If the Auctor had turned their last adventure—mishaps and all—into something good, was there a reason for everything that was happening today, as well? There had to be, Landon thought. At least he hoped so. Although it was difficult to guess a good reason for losing his Bible. Unless. . .

The wheels inside Landon's head were turning.

"Maybe He wants us to see what we can remember," Landon said aloud. Holly was gazing at the sea to the right while Bridget studied the underside of the book where its spine connected to the wood rail.

Landon continued, "I think maybe even losing the Bible, or at least leaving it behind, is to serve some purpose for us. Maybe the Auctor"—Bridget glanced up questioningly—"maybe *God* wants us to see what we know by heart, what we can remember."

Holly turned from the water to look at the sails. Her mouth was moving as her eyes traveled up and down the outstretched cups of cloth. Landon snorted a laugh and shook his head. No harm in counting sails, he figured. She just couldn't help herself.

"I'm listening," she said in the middle of her silent tally. "To see what we know by heart." She squinted. "I wish I could see all the sails up there."

Landon sighed. "So what were the verses we'd read in the lobby, just before the water came pouring in? I'm afraid my mind has gone blank with all that has happened."

Bridget stood and placed both of her hands on the right side of the book. Landon noticed and lifted his right hand over hers and placed it next to his other hand. Now they each held down half of the book, and they glanced at each other and smiled.

"I remember," said Bridget. "It was in Genesis, chapter seven, verses eleven and twelve. It said, 'In the six hundredth year of Noah's life, in the second month, the seventeenth day of the month, the same day were all the fountains of the great deep broken up, and the windows of heaven were opened. And the rain was upon the earth forty days and forty nights.' "

Landon smiled at his little sister again, though his smile had changed to one of awe. "How did you do that?"

"Do what?"

"You remembered that exactly as I read it. And I couldn't remember any of it."

"All the excitement erased your memory, but I guess it pressed the words into mine."

Landon laughed and shook his head. "Amazing." He looked at the billowing sails and licked his lips. Then he grimaced and stuck out his tongue.

"What is it?" asked Bridget. "What's wrong with your face?"

"Nothing," Landon said, and then he laughed. He licked his lips again. "Blah! Salt! My lips are salty."

Bridget licked her lips round and round and rolled her eyes at the same time. She stuck out her tongue, and Landon laughed.

"Can you believe I lost count?" Holly looked at Landon and Bridget. They both stuck out their tongues. Holly rolled her eyes. "Of course it's salty, you guys. We're at sea." She lifted her arms, and as the ship rocked forward, her arms fell and then rose again as the ship rocked back. It looked as if she were trying to fly in slow motion.

"I can't count from up here. I'm going down there to the, to the. . .uh. . ."

"Main deck," said Landon. He was squinting, working on something else. "Brine!" he said suddenly. "They taste *briny.*"

"Aye-aye, matey," said Holly. "I'm going down to count the sails. Who knows? It may come in handy to know these things." About halfway down a short set of stairs (what was it called on a ship—a *ladder*?), Holly paused, grasping a rope on either side of her and leaning forward as the ship rocked, and then leaning back. "One thing's for sure," she hollered without looking back.

"What's that?" Landon shouted down to her.

"I don't think we're in the library anymore!"

After another forward-and-then-backward-leaning pause, Holly hastened down the steps and onto the deck. Once there, she seemed to be getting a feel for the ship's movement, progressing forward as it teetered that way, and then leaning against the tilt as it rocked back. She kept her stance wide, and soon she disappeared beneath the sail.

Sunlight streamed behind the sails, first traveling up and then traveling down among them. Landon realized he and Bridget were standing in the shade. "We're heading west," he said thoughtfully, "into the setting sun." Then he turned to Bridget. "So what else do you remember about Noah and the flood?"

They talked about the animals, of course, pairs of one male and one female of each species. "Like a floating zoo," said Bridget. Landon made a mental note that Holly would be good for counting and keeping track of the animals, though he wasn't sure why this thought even occurred to him.

They talked about the ark—made of cypress wood, wasn't it? Whatever cypress wood was. Sealed with pitch. It had to be big for all those animals. And who was on board with the animals? Noah, of course.

"The captain," said Bridget.

Noah's wife had to be there, and they had sons. . .Sham and Hem—no. Wait. Shem, Ham, and Jethro or Jarpeth or something. Anyway, there were three of them. Did they have wives along? Landon and Bridget looked at each other. They must have, they decided. So there were eight people with all the animals on one big ship.

"Why is it called an ark and not a boat or a ship?" Bridget asked.

"Hmm," said Landon. "*Ark. Ark.* That is a funny word. You know, I don't know. I'd never thought about that."

They knew it had rained for forty days and forty nights, as that was in the passage Landon had read and Bridget had memorized. But the ark was afloat for much longer than forty days, wasn't it? Landon thought it was over a hundred. Bridget wasn't sure. Landon looked at his little sister and said, "You know, this is kind of fun. I don't think I've ever talked about Noah and the ark with anyone before."

Bridget made a funny face, sort of like a frown but not like she was mad. "Landon, why *are* we talking about Noah and the ark and the"—Bridget glanced out to sea—"flood?"

Landon took a deep breath. Well, Bridget was in on this adventure now. He might as well go ahead and explain to her about the others. About his first journey into Wonderwood through the giant *Book of Meanings* and the chessboard and Melech and the whole bit. And then about his and Holly's encounter with the dreadful shadows of Malus Quidam. By the time he finished telling the stories, Bridget looked rather pale and almost green. Landon couldn't tell if it was from shock or disbelief or seasickness. Perhaps all of the above.

"So you see, whatever underlined words we read in the Bible—in my special Bible—before the journey begins, well, they tell us something about the journey." He paused, feeling a sloshing in his own stomach. A belch helped clear it and put him at ease. "I think that's how it happens, anyway."

Bridget still looked rather ill. Her eyes half drooped as if she were tired. Instead of saying she was going to find a place to lie down for a nap, however, she said, "Excuse me," and then turned around and staggered to the railing. There she took hold of it with both hands, leaned her head over, and—

Landon turned away. He didn't want to have to go to the railing himself. His stomach growled, and he realized he was hungry along with feeling a bit queasy. The thought of being on an empty ship in the middle of the sea with no food was not a pleasant one. Not pleasant at all. Landon had both hands on the book now, steady as she goes, and was beginning to wonder where Holly had gone to, when he heard her voice from below.

Chapter Five

"Ahoy, Cap'n!" Holly's voice rang up.

Hey, Landon liked the sound of that. *Cap'n.*

"Ahoy, matey!" he said, promptly burping. "Our shipmate's sick. We could use some help up here."

"Catch!"

A flying sea snake was coming to strangle him! At the last instant, Landon recognized the length of rope Holly had flung up from the main deck. Letting go of the book, he snatched the rope from the air. The ship veered easily to the left as a few pages turned.

"Tie down the helm, Landon, and come down here. Bridget, too! You've got to see this!"

Hey—what happened to *Cap'n*? But Landon nodded and steered the ship straight again by flipping back a few pages. With the rope, he secured the book. No expert at tying knots, he made a modified double bow like he did when lacing up his football shoes.

"You all right?" he asked Bridget. She shook her head. "Can you make it down the steps? Holly wants to show us something." Bridget nodded, and Landon guided her to the ladder and followed her down. The main deck shot before him like a football field. This ship was enormous.

"This way," Holly said. She spun them right around and, after lifting a wooden latch, led them through a doorway and down a short passageway—rocking side to side more than front to back, Landon now noticed—into a good-sized room.

"This must be the captain's quarters," said Holly. "Look. . . a real bed. And check this out. Food and jugs of something, something liquid. And that's not all," she said in a hushed, excited tone. "I went below deck and found more. Lots more. We could live out here for days. Maybe weeks."

Bridget groaned. She was headed straight for the bed. Well, not exactly straight. The ship's rocking had her swerving either direction and even bouncing off the slightly curved wall once before making it to the bed. But Landon wasn't concerned about the bed or even the food at the moment. He had stepped to the back wall, which was more window than wall. It was comprised of rectangles of glass and narrow, crisscrossed beams of dark wood. And as it curved back around him to either side, he stepped into a full panoramic view of the sea behind them. The ship's white wake trailed like a gradually expanding V.

"It's pretty, isn't it?" Holly stood beside him.

"It's beautiful. I've never seen the ocean before."

"I know. None of us have."

Landon and Holly stood quietly, swaying gently back and forth. Back and forth. The only sound was the rhythmic creaking of the ship, which Landon found to be, well, rather *poetic* and soothing. He thought he could also make out the swishing of the water below as it ripped away from the ship. The movement and the soft noise was beginning to lull him into drowsiness. Bridget's wail roused him.

"What?" he said going to the bed. Poor thing. She looked awful.

"I feel terrible," she said. "I think I'm sick."

"She needs food," said Landon, thinking he did too, though not quite as badly.

"Won't she just throw it up?" said Holly.

Landon thought. That was a good point. He looked at Bridget. "Could you keep some food down?" She nodded, though not too convincingly. "What do we have?" he asked Holly. She had gone into a cubbyhole, and Landon could hear scraping and bumping and even metallic sounding clinks that made him think of silverware.

"Here we go." Holly came out with a tray laden with what appeared to be chunks of bread and dried meat. Landon looked at it and then at Holly. She glanced up and shrugged. "It looks okay and"—she bent her head—"smells okay, too."

Landon shrugged and went to the cubbyhole. Crates of fruit were stacked against one side. Shelves on the other side held jugs and mugs and platters and jars and other containers of various foods. Each shelf had a raised lip to hold its contents. It appeared a few items had spilled, presumably from when Landon had closed the book and tipped the whole ship. The shelves were still fairly full, which also helped keep everything in place.

Landon removed a cork-stopped jug and three mugs, setting them outside the cubbyhole. He then lifted a top crate and, after removing three oranges from it, set it alongside the bed as a small table. Holly set the tray there, and Landon brought over the jug and three mugs.

The cork removal made a loud pop, and Landon could hear the jug's contents fizz. "Champagne, anyone?" he said with a grin.

Bridget moaned but then said she could use a good burp.

Holly laughed and said this was kind of fun and this must surely be their best adventure yet. "Well, aside from Bridget being sick. Here, Bridget." Holly gave her sister a peeled orange slice. "Vitamin C prevents colds at least."

"And oranges prevent scurvy, too, I think," said Landon. "The citric acid."

The liquid from the jug was not champagne, of course. It was ginger ale. The food and the drink and the rocking of the ship had all three children belching and giggling in no time. Even poor Bridget eventually started to giggle, and this gave her the hiccups, which caused the three of them to giggle all the more.

After they'd had their fill, Landon corked the jug, and they slid everything back toward the cubbyhole. He went to stand at the vast window. "It's going to get dark soon," he said, already feeling the heaviness of a dark night at sea. "Holly? Did you find any lanterns or candles?"

A sparking match and small flickering light gave him his answer.

"Would you believe I had these matches in my pocket this

whole time?" said Holly.

Landon tried to determine the tone of her voice. Was she kidding? Then he thought about the flood in the library and how they'd all been soaked through.

"No," he said warily. "I don't believe you."

"Well. . .you're right!" She was smiling now, her face visible in the glow of a lantern, which she was hanging on a hook near the bed. "I found them in the pantry." She gestured toward the cubbyhole. "The closet. Whatever you call that. And these matches are weird. They're like little wood sticks that you scrape on this stone."

She was holding something and scraping it with her finger. But Landon's attention was back on the sea out the window. Now that he knew they had a little light inside the ship (and it wasn't lost on him how resourceful Holly proved herself to be. What would they have done without her?), he could relax for the moment and think about the larger situation. The bigger picture as it were. Namely, what were they doing here? Where were they going? And the question he really didn't want to think about quite yet but that was already beginning to niggle at him anyway: *How would they ever get back to Button Up and their family?* Landon didn't even know which ocean they were on, the Atlantic or the Pacific (or the Indian or the Arctic for that matter). So at the moment, he had no way even to guess which direction they should go.

Then the thought struck him, of course, that they may not be on any ocean in our world anyway. This thought made him both excited and a little nervous.

"I'm really glad you guys are with me," said Landon at last.

"I would have liked to see Melech and Vates and Hardy and—"

"That's a horse and an old man and—"

"She knows, Holly. I told her already."

"You did? Oh. Well, I suppose that makes sense."

And, Landon thought, *Ditty.* He gazed at the sea and sighed.

"Landon?" Bridget's voice caused him to look over.

"Yes?"

"How did they find land?"

Landon frowned. "Who?"

"Noah and everybody."

Landon looked back out to sea. "I think land found them, eventually. They came to rest on a mountain or something."

"Oh." Bridget didn't sound too thrilled.

"Didn't they send out a bird first?" said Holly. "I mean, Noah. He sent out a dove and it came back, and then he sent another bird, or maybe it was the dove again, and it came back—"

"With a leaf or branch in its mouth. That's right." Landon nodded, feeling pleased despite the seeming uselessness of this information. Then again, nothing from the Bible was useless. Even the parts that didn't seem to make sense.

"And the third time a bird went out—and this time I'm pretty sure it *wasn't* a dove—and, well, it didn't ever come back."

"I know," Bridget said in a whimpering voice. "That's so sad."

"What do you mean?"

"The bird never came back. What about its wife or husband, the other bird it left on the ark? I think it's sad," Bridget reaffirmed.

"Well, it meant that the bird found land," explained Holly. "So when the ark landed, then the two birds found each other again."

"Are you sure? Why did the birds have to wait until the ark landed? Couldn't they all fly off early so those two birds could be together again?"

"Oh, Bridget," Holly said.

Landon smiled. "Too bad we don't have a bird. I guess we'll just have to wait for land to find *whuuusss*!" He stumbled toward the bed and grabbed it, finding himself staring at the lantern, which hung straight despite the tilting of everything around it.

"The book!" exclaimed Holly. "Didn't you tie it?"

"Yes!" Landon was already climbing toward the passageway. "But I'm no good with knots."

Something clattered at the far, upturned end of the room and came rolling speedily toward Landon. He wanted to get out of its way but knew he wouldn't make it. So Landon reached out and caught the thing, surprised at his own quickness under these conditions. It was brass—smooth and round and tubular. At first, Landon thought it was some sort of old, strange flash-light. The brass gleamed in the dimming light. But then Landon noticed the end opposite the lens also held a lens, although a much smaller one. As he lifted it, the smaller end fell out twice—*click, click!* It was a small telescope. "Cool," said Landon crawling through the passageway.

"Hurry!" Holly yelled. "Bridget's about to fall out of bed!"

Collapsing the sections back together, Landon stuffed the telescope into his back pocket and climbed the ladder to the bridge.

The book had indeed closed.

And the rope was missing.

Landon opened the cover and turned page after page after page until the ship was steadily plowing straight ahead. This was going to be a long night if he had to stay up here watching the book. He guessed that's how life must be on board a ship. Someone always had to man the wheel, as it were. He might as well take the first watch. Or shift. How did the driver know how to steer though, with the sails all in the way? Did they raise the sails at night? And how could he and Holly manage that?

Landon looked up, and a new sense of awe overcame him. The sky had become a broad rainbow, stretching from dark red in the west to a deep blue behind them. That was the grand finale to the story of Noah and the ark, wasn't it? A rainbow banding the sky and God promising Noah that He would never flood the earth again?

Yes.

So, Landon figured, there must be land out there somewhere. *He promised.* It couldn't all be water, could it? Unless the promise didn't cover *this* world, wherever this was.

Holly emerged atop the ladder. "Thought you could use another one." She handed him an orange. "And I found this on the deck." She held out the rope. "It must have blown down from a crosswind or something. Bridget's sleeping."

Landon laughed. "Sleeping. . .that's our Bridget. And a crosswind, huh?" He took the orange but shrugged off the rope. "You're sounding more and more like a sailor all the time." He grinned at Holly.

Holly intertwined the rope with the top of the railing, tying it at each end. Her knots looked better than Landon's, though neither of them said anything.

"And you're looking more like one," she said sizing up her brother.

"Like what?" Landon held the orange against the book with his body and took hold of the front and back covers, setting his face to the wind with a swarthy squint.

"A sailor, silly."

Landon smiled.

"What's that in your pocket?"

"Oh yeah. Could you take the helm, First Mate? I want to check this out."

"First Mate? Is that like being Second-to-None?" Holly stepped in and took the book in her hands.

"Not at all," said Landon. "It's better." He took out the telescope and extended it. As he set it to his eye, however, the ship lurched and Landon almost tumbled right into Holly against the helm. "What was that?" he said, realizing the book was still open and they hadn't dipped at all to the right or left. "It felt like you hit the brakes."

"It couldn't be land," Holly said, just as perplexed. "Could it?"

"Land," said Landon under his breath. "I don't think so. We're still gliding, aren't we? Hey—look."

Holly looked to where Landon was pointing. The sails hung completely limp. Holly gasped. "The wind," she said softly, almost as if someone else might be listening. "It's stopped."

"Weird," said Landon.

The colors were fading from the sky. Only a faint rim of

red clung to the horizon. "Red sky at night," Landon uttered, "sailors' delight." They wouldn't have to worry about a midnight storm at least, if the old adage held true.

Landon remembered the telescope. "I'm going to take a quick look around before it's too dark." He walked out on the bridge wing and held the scope up to his eye. The horizon zoomed closer. But there was nothing more to see really, only dimming sky and gently swelling water topped by a faint pink mist.

Landon moved from where the sun was setting and continued to scan the horizon to his right. "Looking north," he said to himself. "And now east. . ." He was looking behind the ship. He was about to swing southward and then around to a close-up of Holly when he felt an electric thrill run through him. Landon paused, trying to hold the telescope steady. Slowly he brought it back around to the east, to the spread of sea behind the ship.

The sky was already getting dark, and the sea even darker. Stars were appearing. Was that it? The stars? Had he seen a familiar constellation? "Hmm," he muttered. "Not sure. . ."

"What's that?"

"Nothing, Holly." Landon tried to concentrate. "I don't think there's anything but wa—"

After a long pause, Holly said, "But wa—water? But what?"

"Wait," said Landon. He gazed through the circle. Where was it? He watched as stars seemed to glow brighter by the moment. Starlight began to softly twinkle off the water. There was something else. Something that wasn't stars or reflected starlight. Something where the light was completely missing.

"What is it?" said Holly, her voice growing tighter. "Landon?"

"I see a shape," said Landon doubtfully. His heart began to pound. He licked the salt from his lips and swallowed. "I see a ship, Holly. And I think it's following us."

Landon noted the stillness of the air and the limp sails. “I’d give anything for a speedboat right now,” he said. The ship rocked gently. As the water slowly rippled past, it was hard to tell which was moving more, the ship or the sea. “Not much we can do without a motor or,” he added wryly, “some really long oars.”

Holly was pacing the deck. She paused, squinting at the vast sea behind them. “May I?” She held out her hand.

Landon placed the spyglass into her hand. “Sure.” As Holly surveyed the scene, Landon thought she looked even more anxious than he was feeling.

“I see it,” Holly said quietly. After a long while, she slowly raised the scope until it was almost vertical. Her hair hung low as she arched her back. Slowly, she drew the scope back down.

“What are you doing?” asked Landon. He didn’t think she could be gauging the mysterious ship’s distance from them. Then again, Holly was pretty brilliant when it came to mathematical equations in any form.

"I'd guess," said Holly slowly, apparently working out something in her head, "it will catch us by morning. Unless the wind picks up. That would be to our advantage." Again she raised and lowered the telescope, her mouth moving silently. "Yes, I would say it's gaining on us. And. . .weird. . ."

"What?" Landon was itching to take back the telescope. "What is it?"

"Well, I don't see any sails or masts. Although it is hard to tell from this far and in the dark."

"What are you," asked Landon, "a hawk? How can you see that? Give me the telescope."

"Just a sec—"

"Holly."

"All right, all right. I just want to see which side of our ship they'll probably come up on." Holly lowered the telescope and sighed. Something heavy seemed to be on her mind.

"We'll get back to Button Up somehow," said Landon feigning confidence. How? And when? He had no idea. He thought it important to have faith, however, and to put on a good show of it for his sisters.

"That's not what I'm worried about." Holly heaved another sigh.

"What are you worried about, then?"

When Holly looked at him, Landon suddenly felt that she and he were much older than their eleven and twelve respective years. "There's something else down below," said Holly. "Three levels down."

Landon waited, turning the end piece of the telescope. "And. . . ?" he added coaxingly. This was unlike Holly. Usually she couldn't wait to share her discoveries. Even if something was supposed to be a secret, such as Landon's animal vision during the football game. Landon's breathing quickened. He stopped twirling the telescope lens. "What, Holly? What did you find?" Each passing second made Landon's heart beat harder.

"Um," she said finally, obviously struggling to get it out. Her face tightened into a frown. She looked concerned, perplexed, and slightly afraid. "I found weapons." She looked down and then lifted her eyes meekly as if she'd done something wrong. "A whole—what do you call it?—a stash of them."

Landon's heart continued to hammer. A stash of weapons? On board his ship?

My ship, he thought with a little smile.

"You mean a *cache* of weapons," he said. "Well, you know I've got to get to the bottom of this. What kind of weapons?"

Holly raised her eyebrows. "Want me to show you?"

Landon tried to swallow as casually as possible, though it felt like he was gulping down a stone. Slowly, he nodded. "Yes," he squeaked. He cleared his throat. "Yes, of course. Let's go."

After examining the distant ship through the scope and muttering "No sails. Hmm. . ." to himself, Landon pretended to test Holly's knots securing the book, and then he headed down the ladder behind her. They found two lanterns—they weren't about to go below deck in the dark—and went through a hatch and down a ladder. Landon caught a dim glimpse of a room with some tables and stools, apparently for eating at. Holly said more food and even a crude kitchen were at the far end of the room.

"The galley," said Landon. "Amazing."

They found a door that Holly hadn't discovered. After looking at each other a moment, they pushed through and found a number of hammocks strung between poles. Three huge poles spanned the long room, recognizable as the ship's masts. Planks all about them creaked as the ship lolled first to one side and then back to the other. The hammocks accentuated the ship's movement, hanging fairly still like so many white pea pods. Such a vast space obviously meant for people to sleep in gave Landon a strange feeling. "It's so. . .empty," he whispered.

"I don't think I want to sleep down here," said Holly.

"Unh-uh." Landon shook his head. "No way. Gives me the creeps."

"Come on."

Holly led the way back out and down a narrow passageway, where another hatch in the deck opened to a ladder.

"You came down here by yourself?" Landon asked in amazement.

"It was daylight," Holly said. "And it was actually light down here somehow. I think there were windows in the room with the galley."

"Portholes," said Landon.

"Yeah, little round windows. And down here, too, there was light. Though not as much."

Landon looked down the dark hole. "May I?" he asked bravely.

Holly smiled. "Please."

It was tricky going down with one hand holding a lantern. When Landon reached the bottom, he reached up for Holly's lantern so she could more easily descend the final steps.

"Be careful," Holly said, "not to drop the lanterns."

"Well, I wasn't exactly intending to, Holly."

"I know. But especially not over there."

Landon snorted but then caught his breath. Nearly touching his right hip was the solid rounded casing of—

"A cannon," said Landon holding Holly's lantern out to her. He touched the cold metal and flinched, drawing back his finger as if his mere touch might set the thing off. An iron loop at the rear of the cannon had a thick rope tied to it like a tail. Outside the ship, the sea was sloshing. The waterline must only be several feet below. The ominous row of cannons ran on into the darkness.

"Ten on each side," said Holly, who of course had counted them earlier.

And then Landon saw why Holly had said not to drop a lantern. Circling a center mast was a ring of wooden barrels, secured by a rope and coated in black dust.

Landon stared, tightening his grip on the lantern handle. "Gun powder?"

"It appears so," said Holly.

"Are there any guns?"

"Didn't see any. I mean, besides those big ones," she said, referring to the cannons. "But look over here."

Landon had a hard time looking away from the barrels. He glanced back at the cannons and then noticed where light would have been coming in earlier. An open square in front of one of the cannons faced the outside. This also explained the loud whooshing of the sea.

A metallic *clink* sounded, and Landon turned. Holly stood a ways beyond the ladder, holding something shiny. With the ship's next creaking tilt, Landon stepped over to find his sister clutching a long, steel sword. As she slid the sword back into a cratelike case, it rattled against the wood from her trembling. The case appeared to hold about fifty swords. Along the left side of the ship, more cannons loomed.

"So this is the cache." Landon carefully lifted a sword and soon discovered why Holly's arm was trembling. The thing was surprisingly heavy. Landon found a hook on the wall and, after tugging it to make sure it held, hung his lantern. With two hands, the sword was more manageable. He could fit both his hands within the curved handle. A thrill ran through Landon's body. This was like grasping a bat to take a few practice swings before stepping up to the plate. Except this felt much more—powerful. And dangerous.

Landon eyed the blade up and down. It was all he could do to keep from waving it around. Apparently sensing his enthusiasm, Holly had retreated a few steps. Finally, and with some reluctance, Landon slid the weapon back into its place.

Holly stepped nearer. "Is this a pirate ship, do you think?"

Landon lifted his lantern from the hook. "Was a pirate ship, maybe. Except. . ."

He tilted his head as something on the sword's hilt caught his eye. Leaning closer, Landon held the lantern over the sword. "Look at this, Holly."

Holly leaned in and held her lantern as a bookend to Landon's, their faces between the gently swaying lights.

Landon read the inscription—"B.G.B."—and looked at Holly with wide eyes.

She gasped. Her nose almost brushed his when she turned.

"Landon! Is it? Is this? I mean, was this—?"

"It was his sword, Holly, but not his ship. Look at the bottom of the handle—well, the top now." He rose a little, lifting his lantern.

Each sword handle had been stamped on the bottom: U.S.N. Bartholomew's initials on the side of the hilt were crudely engraved, as if scraped by hand. The U.S.N. letters, however, were centered and uniform on every sword.

Landon smiled, thrilling by the minute.

Holly frowned. "So what does that mean, U.S.N.?"

Relishing the moment, Landon took a deep breath and slowly exhaled. It felt so good to have figured this out. Especially when Holly was still in the dark.

"Old Bart wasn't a pirate, though I'm sure he would have made a fine one." Landon squinted, pursing his lips. He tried imagining Bart in a pirate's hat with an eye patch and a parrot clawed on his shoulder. *Aaargh!* Instead of a silver hook for a hand, however, Bart probably would have been holding a fishing hook. Landon snorted a laugh.

"So," said Holly, an agitated edge to her voice. "What was he? And whose ship—wait a second. Oh. . ." Her voice rose and fell away.

Landon's heart sank. Had she really figured it out, too?

"So he was a Viking?"

Landon laughed. "No! I don't think so. And I don't think they had cannons, anyway."

Holly frowned again. Finally, she shrugged her shoulders. "Well, smarty-pants, what was he then? And whose ship was this?"

Landon's chest swelled with pride. Even more than figuring out old Bart's former occupation, he was happy to realize that Bart wasn't only a hermit who loved to fish and read. He had another side that Grandpa Karl had never let on about in his telling of the legend. Bartholomew G. Benneford had also been a patriot.

"He was a sailor," said Landon.

Holly's frown remained, and she half rolled her eyes. "Well, we're sailors now, aren't we? I mean, we're sailing on a ship."

Landon didn't deflate. "Yeah, but he was a *real* sailor, Holly. He served in the United States Navy." As Landon waited for his sister to be impressed, the vessel around them creaked one way, paused, and then groaned to the other side.

Holly was considering. "Did they even have a navy back then?"

Landon sighed. She was brilliant with numbers, to be sure. But Holly sorely needed to brush up on her history.

"Of course they did. *We* did. Our country's had a navy since the Revolutionary War. You haven't heard about John Paul Jones?"

Holly shook her head. Then she brightened. "I did see that picture of George Washington crossing a river in a boat. But"—she glanced around—"his boat was more like the size of this when it was a tombstone."

The ship lurched, and both children stumbled back a few steps, holding out their lanterns. "Maybe the wind's picking up," said Landon. "We'd better check on Bridget. And the book."

He was standing behind the space between two cannons on the left side of the ship. An open crate sat between the guns. It was full of black balls the size of baseballs. Landon picked one up and almost tipped over with it. It weighed more than a bowling ball. "Whoa," he said, dropping it back in with the others. In a rack along the wall hung two poles. One had a hook at one end and an odd, squarish scoop at the other. The second pole had a black cylinder at one end, making it look like a giant swab.

The ship rocked unsteadily again. Beyond the grating and groaning of wood, Landon thought he might have heard a human moan. "Let's go check on her."

Up in the captain's cabin, Bridget still lay asleep, much to Landon's relief. However, the bed covers were pulled away and loose. Either Bridget had been tossing and turning from restlessness, or the ship's heaving had rolled her about. Landon noted that a storm at sea would render the bed rather useless. Its occupant would surely tumble to the floor.

Drowsiness was creeping into Landon, and he became aware of the weight of his eyelids.

"She seems okay," said Landon.

Holly gently stroked Bridget's hair and nodded. For a moment, Landon had the impression he and Holly were the parents and Bridget the little girl. Well she *was* the little girl, their little sister. And they would take care of her.

Landon fought off a yawn. He had too much responsibility to be tired. "I'm going to check on that ship. Maybe it's gone away now." Part of him was hoping that it hadn't gone away, however. For now, the distant ship remained a mysterious excitement more than a dangerous threat.

"Are you going up to the bridge?"

Landon hadn't even thought about it. He *was* getting tired. Being at sea, he decided, was exhausting. "I can check right here," he said. "From the window."

"Good," said Holly. With night settling in, apparently she wasn't so keen on being alone anymore. Landon appreciated her presence, too, and thought it good for the three of them to be together.

Planting his feet wide, Landon removed the spyglass from his back pocket and extended it. The horizon was surprisingly easy to make out, especially through the scope. The path directly behind their ship was clear, and Landon felt his heart sinking a bit. The thought occurred to him that maybe before he had only seen a mirage or a blind spot on the water. Then he almost giggled at himself, realizing that a blind spot wasn't something you saw but a spot where you *couldn't* see.

But Holly had seen it too, right? Could they both have seen the same mirage?

"Boy. I *am* going to have to sleep. I can hardly hold up this telescope."

"What?" said Holly. She sat by the bed, eating an orange slice.

Landon shook his head despite himself. "Nothing." Forcing himself to finish scanning the horizon—he had to make sure, didn't he?—Landon swept the telescope toward the left until the edge of the window came startlingly into view. He lowered the scope for a moment, rested his eyes, and then raised it again. Starting at the left edge of the window, he peered through the circle, closing his left eye, and then stopped. He took a step forward to gain a better view to the left. His heart skipped at what he saw, and he was suddenly a little bit more awake.

"Holly."

"Yeah?"

"You were right."

Holly waited.

"It'll catch us by morning. In fact, it's almost catching us now."

So much for wanting the mystery and excitement. What had been a distant curiosity was now a disturbing reality closing in.

Unfortunately, the wind had not picked up. The sudden lurches they'd felt earlier had apparently only been from rogue waves. They were stuck. They were—Landon swallowed a lump in his throat—*dead in the water.*

Bridget let out a little moan. Perhaps she could sense the approaching danger in her sleep. Should they wake her? No, not yet. She wasn't well, and at least one of them was getting some rest. Landon closed his eyes and let his chin drop. *Come on,* he prayed. *Just one little breath. One tiny puff from You, and we'll be sailing free and clear again. Blow us out of here!* Landon puffed his own cheeks and blew as if willing the wind to blow on a larger scale outside.

The ship rocked gently as before.

"Landon?"

He lifted his head and glanced at Holly. Even their lanterns were growing dim. He squinted against the darkness.

"If this *isn't* a pirate ship—I mean, if it belongs to the navy—then what do you suppose that other ship is?"

"I don't know," he said. "I just hope they're friendly." The pounding of his heart suggested otherwise.

Holly stood and came over next to him. She stared out the window. "Where—oh, there it is." A slight pause. "At least this way it still looks kind of far away. I mean, without the telescope."

She was right, of course. Though the ship's dark outline was now visible to the naked eye upon the faintly shimmering black water, it was still a distance away. The telescope brought it dreadfully close.

"What if it's like this ship?" said Holly. They were both gazing at it now. The lanterns had practically gone out.

"What do you mean?" said Landon.

"I mean, what if it's empty? Like a ghost ship."

Somehow this thought made it seem worse, not better. "Great," said Landon. "Thanks for putting that in my head. Being chased by a ghost ship. I think I'd rather face pirates."

"I keep thinking about all those empty hammocks down below. And the swords and the cannons. And even this room. I mean. . ." Holly shuddered.

"I know," said Landon. The thought wasn't lost on him that this ship had formerly been a tombstone, albeit one shaped like a rowboat. "I hadn't wanted to go below earlier because. . ."

Holly looked at him.

Landon sighed. It was sad to admit that, by exploring the ship alone, his sister had been braver than he. Holly could be rather courageous at times. She could also be rather reckless.

"You thought you'd find ghosts?" she asked.

Landon snorted. "No. Skeletons."

Holly shivered again, hugging her arms. "Oh my. I'm glad I *hadn't* thought of those. I don't think I would have gone down there then."

Landon shoved the telescope in his back pocket and put his arm around his sister. "I had forgotten one important thing, though." He felt Holly's shivering calm, and he went on. "We're not alone on this ship, Holly. But it's not because of skeletons or ghosts from the navy."

Though he hadn't been shivering himself, Landon found comfort in his own words. Sometimes it helped to speak these things aloud. "The Auctor is with us," he said simply. "He knows we're here, because he's here, too."

Landon was aware of both their bodies swaying with the ship. The mysterious vessel behind them loomed close as ever. Yet it didn't seem so threatening now. *The Auctor is with us.*

"You really believe that," said Holly, "don't you? That there's one who knows everything and who's really in charge. Even when it seems like no one is."

Landon was surprised, not by his sister's doubt, if she did doubt, but more by the depth and grown-up tone of their conversation.

"Yeah," he said. "Yes, I do. I can't help believing in him, really. Plus, I think I *want* to believe in him. Don't you?"

Holly was nodding. "Yeah," she said staring out the huge window. "Especially now."

"Especially now," Landon echoed softly. He found he was smiling and feeling profoundly tired again. With a new lightness and confidence in his heart, Landon decided he would go ahead and get some sleep. If he *could* sleep. The Auctor would waken him when the time was right.

"I'm going to go out and get some fresh air. Breathe some of that salty sea breeze. What breeze there is, anyway."

"Are you going to the bridge?"

"I'll check on the book, though it feels like it's okay. Then I'm going to look for a spot on the deck somewhere. Sleep under the stars."

"How romantic," said Holly dryly. "You're not going down below to the hammocks?" She arched her eyebrows at him.

"Uh, no. I don't think so. It's the sails and stars for me."

"Uh-huh. Well, I might lie on the bed here with Bridget. Though I hope I don't get sick."

"Seasickness isn't contagious. As long as you don't see her throw—you know." Landon puffed his cheeks and made an urping sound.

Holly pulled away. "Thanks." She yawned broadly. "Sweet dreams."

"You, too."

Landon watched as Holly climbed carefully into the bed. Bridget moaned and turned away. He stepped through the short passageway and opened the door to the deck. Between the rear mast and the center mast, somewhat shielded by the limp sails overhead, he did find a large net piled back and forth on top of itself. It wasn't the most comfortable bed in the world, but when he laid down on it, his weary body didn't seem to care. He laced his fingers behind his head and gazed at the stars beyond the sails and masts and round crow's nest at the top. The stars rolled together one way, stalled, and then rolled back the other way. That sight along with the faint *swoosh* of the sea and the salty air soon lulled Landon to sleep. The last thing he was aware of was the sensation that the entire world was gently rocking. . . .

Gently rocking. . .

Gently rocking. . .

In Landon's dream, he saw two ships at sea, one chasing after the other. But then the sea became a floor of dark and light squares. A giant chessboard. The ships were chess pieces: one, a knight, and the other, a queen. The queen was after the knight, pursuing it toward the corner of the board. And then Landon was on the knight, and they were bounding, bounding forward two squares, then lurching to the left. Then forward two more squares and lurching to the right. The back-and-forth motion was slightly nauseating. It was also exhilarating. The knight stopped.

"You may get off here. You'll be all right."

Landon couldn't move. He felt extremely heavy, almost glued to the back of the knight's head.

"I said you may get off now. Get off. Get off!"

Except the last *Get off!* sounded more like *Get up!*

"Get up. Get up!"

Landon opened his eyes and immediately closed them again. This time, he opened them more slowly, squinting. He lifted his right arm, which felt like lead, and shielded his eyes from the brightness above. Where in the world was he? And what were those big sheets doing overhead?

He remembered where he was and sat up. His back was so stiff that for a moment he thought *it* was making the loud creaking noise he heard. But it was the ship around him and beneath him that was creaking. Groaning. Rolling. The remnants of Landon's dream and the reality about him collided, and Landon fairly shouted, "I will stand fast and await my fate. I will do my duty and be glad for it!"

Yes, a ship had been chasing them, or at least following them and closing in. And he would do his duty and protect his sisters, whatever that might mean. Landon rolled his tongue around his mouth. What he could really use was a toothbrush and some toothpaste.

Soft footsteps sounded on the deck, and two figures approached from the rear of the ship. They fairly staggered to the right as the ship rolled, and then they emerged beneath the sail.

"Holly," Landon said. "Bridget. Good morn—"

They briefly glanced his way but didn't seem to notice him. They were staring off to his left, beyond the right side of the ship. Landon's arms and legs worked to get him up, but he stumbled and fell back down. What was this stuff he'd been laying on? *Let go of me!* he wanted to shout. It was clingy netting, like a mess of spider webs. Landon eventually scrambled out and stiffly stepped away, walking groggily toward the right side of the ship. Shielding his eyes from the brightness, Landon joined his sisters at the rail. Viewed from the side, Bridget no longer looked green, but both she and Holly appeared chalky white. Landon had thought they were going to the rail because Bridget was still sick, or maybe both of them were. Neither of them was throwing up, however; they were simply staring off to sea. Landon looked at them. Could they be sleepwalking? He was about to ask what was wrong when something caught his eye out on the water.

Despite the glaring sun, Landon opened his eyes wide, grabbed the railing with both hands, and gasped. The mystery ship had caught up with them. But it was no ordinary ship.

Now Landon wondered if *he* was sleepwalking or dreaming or seeing things. Could this be possible? Was he really seeing what it appeared he was seeing?

Then he remembered: the Bible. They had been reading his Bible at the library. *What were we reading? In Genesis. The flood. Noah. . .*

Something released inside him, and one word came out. "Impossible."

"Incredible," said Holly, her voice floating with the gentle breeze that ruffled her hair but did little to the still drooping sails.

Bridget made a sound next, and that's all it was: a sound. Then she spoke real words. "What is it? What happened? Where are we?"

Landon swallowed, wondering what kind of time-travel miracle had happened to get them here. As far as what they were looking at and where they were, well, he had two answers.

"We're at sea," said Landon, stating the obvious. The next part seemed just as obvious yet not so easy to admit. "And that. . ." he said slowly, "is Noah's ark."

The three of them stared at it. What else was there to do?

The ship—or ark, rather—had caught up with them and was sailing—though with no visible sails—a parallel course. This meant that it was hardly moving forward at all and was simply floating as they were and in the same direction.

Landon felt something pressing against the right side of his rear end. He shook his right leg distractedly, thinking maybe it had gone to sleep or was still really stiff. When he reached back to feel it, he touched a cool metal tube. "Argh," he said, reacting to having slept on the thing all night. Then he said, "Ah," and brought the telescope to his eye. As he extended it, the ark grew larger. It was definitely unlike any other seafaring vessel he had ever seen. Then again, he'd never actually seen any ships in person before, only in pictures.

The ark appeared fairly as he had imagined it from drawings and paintings, only much more—well—*real.* It was all of brown wood, though not dark brown. The top half, in fact, appeared quite a bit lighter than the bottom, perhaps bleached by the sun. It was big and tall—extending high over the water—and simple. It could almost be taken for a gargantuan rowboat if not for the little houselike structure on top with the roof.

"Amazing," said Landon. He noted two rows of dark squares running nearly the length of the ark near the top of the body. "There are more windows than I'd thought."

"Windows?" said Holly.

"Animals have to breathe, I suppose," said Landon. The statement sounded funny after he'd said it, but none of them laughed.

"Does this mean," Holly started and then paused. "Does this mean we'll be at sea. . .150 days?"

"I thought it was only forty," Bridget said quietly. It almost sounded like she was speaking to herself. "Forty days and forty nights. . ."

"That was the rain," said Landon. "It rained for forty days, and then—I forget how many days the water stayed."

"At least the rain's over," Holly said. Then she sighed.

Landon lowered the scope and looked at the sky. Above them it was clear and blue, a very bright blue that appeared pale compared to the deep blue of the sea. Beyond the ark, however, clouds were piled all along the horizon, rising up like towers here and there. *Cumulonimbus,* Landon thought. Those must have been the clouds that dumped all the rain.

Landon glanced at the ark again and shook his head. Could they really be back in time, in Noah's day? That would mean they were some of the only people alive on the whole earth. The thought made Landon feel very sad and alone.

"I'm hungry," said Bridget.

Landon thought about what food they had on board, suddenly nervous about rationing it over 150 days.

"We have oranges," said Holly.

"And bread," said Landon. What else was there?

"Toast?" Bridget said hopefully.

"Bread," said Landon.

"Oh."

"They must have a lot of food over there," said Holly. Neither she nor Bridget seemed to have removed their eyes from the astonishing ark. "All those animals to feed."

Again, Landon thought that, in a different situation, those words might have sounded funny. He thought about what kind of funny comeback he might have made, such as, "Well, they better keep the cats away from the mice!" or, "At least the fishing's good."

The fishing!

He looked down at the water swooshing against the ship and then slipping away in a frothy foam. "We might have to catch fish," he said. "There's a big net back there. It's the water I'm mostly worried about."

The girls actually broke their stares and glanced at him.

Landon studied them. "The *drinking* water," he said. He pointed at the sea. "I don't think we can drink that. It'd make us sick."

"No drinking water," said Holly in a monotone, "but ginger ale."

"Oh yeah," said Landon. "The ginger ale then. We may have to drink it sparingly."

Bridget squinted. "Spare-ring-ly?"

"Just a little at a time. Make it last."

"I'm hungry."

Landon smiled. "Let's all go have some breakfast." He thought about something Vates had once said. "It's not good to plan or prepare on an empty stomach. And we may have some planning and preparing to do if—"

Landon caught himself and frowned.

"If what?" asked Bridget.

Landon and Holly looked at each other.

"If we're going to survive," they both said.

The girls turned from the railing and headed for the captain's quarters. Landon watched them go, a new sense of responsibility swelling within him. *We are going to survive.* He was determined to see himself and his sisters through this. Holly could count up all the foodstuffs they had on board, as well as the drinking jugs. Landon would make a more thorough investigation of the entire ship to see just what they had to work with for materials and resources. The challenge of figuring out how to catch and prepare fish to eat was already exciting him. And maybe, he thought, he could even figure out a way to make seawater drinkable. *Then we could survive out here. . .forever.*

He sighed. Forever was a mighty long time. All of a sudden, 150 days didn't sound so bad.

The girls were gone for breakfast. Amazing how quickly you could get used to something—like seeing Noah's ark from your own ship at sea, for instance—and decide to go off for some food. Landon's own stomach was growling and about to pull him away, too. But he had to linger for another good look.

Was it his imagination, or had the ark drifted a bit closer to them? Landon had accepted that the ark was actually there. He could plainly see it even now, and last night he had seen it behind them as a dark silhouette in the distance. What he had a hard time comprehending, though, was what would be inside the ark. If it really was Noah's ark, and it sure appeared to be, then that would mean it was brim full with animals. All sorts of animals. Animals of literally every kind. A giant floating zoo. It would also mean that Noah and his family were aboard.

Landon swallowed. *I could meet Noah. . .in person!* His knees nearly buckled, and it wasn't from the rocking of the ship.

Landon raised the telescope and peered through it. The ark did appear closer; the two-tone brown vessel nearly filled the circular view. As if to satisfy Landon's wish right then, a man appeared on the ark.

Though the ark loomed huge in the scope, the figure of the man was quite small, and only the top half of him was visible. Landon thought he could make out a head of white hair and a white beard. He appeared to be wearing a simple brown robe. Was he holding a staff? His other arm came up and waved. Landon froze. Was the man—was Noah of the Bible—waving at him?

But he wasn't waving *hello.* Rather, his arm only flapped up and down a few times, and then he raised it as if he were pointing. A tiny dot seemed to float away from the man—

It's Noah, Landon thought. *It's gotta be him!*

And that thought triggered the next one.

The dot was a bird. Noah had just released a raven or a dove. He was looking for land!

Holly! Bridget! Landon wanted to scream. He tried to scream. *Come back! It's him—it's Noah!*

He couldn't move. He could scarcely breathe, even though his jaw was hanging open like a cave.

The bird, he thought. *Find the bird. . . .*

He had to pull the spyglass away to scan the sky. Where had the bird gone? The sky was clean, clear blue. Something attracted his attention from below. And it was flying! But Landon's heart sank as he watched a flying fish sail into a wave like a dart. It wasn't alone. Several more flying fish shot from the water, fins flashing like wings, and then disappeared again, engulfed by a wave. Normally, Landon would have been thrilled by such a sight—and the realization that, yes, there were indeed fish in this ocean to catch and eat (though he'd never considered eating a flying one before). But he had a bird to find. A bird! Not a fish.

He looked back at the sky. The bird could have flown off in any direction. With a sigh, Landon gazed back at the ark. Noah was waving again. This time he was waving hello.

"Holly, Bridget," Landon said, though not nearly loud enough to actually be heard by anyone. "Hey guys, I'm waving at Noah." And he was indeed waving his whole arm back and forth, feeling both foolish and exhilarated. When the ship dipped, he had to grab the railing to steady himself. His knees were still a little weak. With a firm grip on the rail, Landon raised the spyglass. One last look, he thought, and then he'd go to settle his growling stomach. Noah appeared to be yelling something.

Instinctively, Landon let go of the rail and cupped his ear. "What?" he said, that same sheepish-yet-ecstatic sensation fluttering through his bones. "I can't hear you, Noah!" Landon grabbed the rail and smiled. He was almost having a conversation with Noah. Breakfast could wait a while longer.

A sound startled him. It wasn't Noah's voice. It was something from the air. What was that? Where was that? Landon's heart rate shifted into yet another gear. As his eyes searched the sky anew, his mind began to reel. *I've heard that sound before.* The next time it came, it was a little louder, clearer, shriller.

"Twee-too! Twee-too!"

A bird swooped and soared, dropped and then climbed. It was coming straight at him. Before Landon knew it, a little green bird had alighted on the railing near his hand. He stared at it, dumbfounded, as it stared keenly back up at him.

"Epops?"

The bird cocked its head and chirped. "Twee-too!"

Landon looked across the water at the ark. "Vates?"

Epops hopped up and down. "Twee-too! Twee-too!"

Landon suddenly wanted to cry, but not because Noah was gone. Because his old friend was here.

Holly and Bridget returned to the deck with an orange and a piece of bread.

"Thanks," said Landon. He introduced Epops to Bridget, and Bridget to the bird. Holly watched the bird in wonder as it danced between the railing and the deck, pecking at the bread crumbs Landon was tossing for it.

"Unbelievable," said Holly. She sounded relieved. Landon, too, was feeling relieved, even though meeting Noah (and seeing all those animals, as well as Noah's family) would have been really, really fantastic.

"Maybe we won't be out here for 150 days after all," Landon said.

"I sure hope not," said Holly. "Orange-slice sandwiches with ginger ale"—she paused to let out a soft belch—"excuse me, would get old really fast." She burped again. "They already are."

As soon as Landon introduced Bridget to Epops, the two seemed to hit it off. Giggling and squealing, Bridget was jumping playfully along the deck after the bird as it flitted between the railing and the ropes. Bridget's voice soared so high, it sounded as if she had inhaled helium.

"I think Bridget's found a new friend," said Holly, smiling.

Bridget had pounced and was squatting like a frog. Suddenly she leaped, clapping and lunging toward the railing as Epops darted deftly out of reach.

Landon laughed. "And she seems to be over her seasickness, too."

"Say, speaking of new friends, look who we have here."

Holly was pointing over the rail but not at the ark, which seemed again to be drifting closer. Landon was glad.

Between the ark and their ship appeared a boat rising and falling with the swells. It was headed their way. The boat was small compared to the ark or the ship. For a rowboat, however, it was pretty good-sized.

Landon's heart couldn't take much more excitement for the day. When he saw who was in the rowboat, however, he felt like it was Christmas and his birthday all rolled into one.

Hardy was at the oars, propelling the craft like an expert boatman. Two others sat in the front; Landon recognized them as people from Wonderwood. Trumplestump and Wagglewhip, perhaps?

Someone else stood in the rear of the boat. Not a person, but a dark horse. The horse appeared a bit awkward, rising and falling with the waves. Yet he somehow looked dignified and steadfast, too.

Landon couldn't help himself. A tear dripped from his eye, and a lump formed in his throat.

Melech.

He had to think the name through a couple times before his voice could manage it. "Melech," he said softly. Then, "Melech!"

The horse began to whinny and raised his head, which dropped abruptly with the next dip in the sea. Everyone was here then it seemed, except—

Clank! Crack-thump. . .scraaape—clank!

Over the ship's rail sailed two heavy hooks trailing rope. Once the hooks had dug into the base of the railing and were latched, up shimmied the two less familiar men from the valley. They climbed on board, and suddenly Landon's ship didn't feel so empty anymore.

The two stocky men began lowering two ropes over the side through pulleys that were rigged to the ship. The bottom of each rope held a large brass hook. Landon hadn't even noticed the pulleys before. The men wore boots beneath their rolled-up trousers. Their light-colored shirts appeared stained and dirty. Each had on a vest, one red and the other black. The one with the red vest wore a three-pointed black hat; the other, a similar red hat. The hats weren't large enough for pirates. Instead, they gave the squat, sturdy men the appearance of two short Paul Reveres.

"Ho, Hardy, ho!"

"Not yet!" Hardy's voice rose from the boat below. "Okay den. Heave! Horsey away!"

The two men groaned and pulled. Melech rose in fits and starts. It was hard to appear very dignified in his current condition. Hardy had affixed a broad white harness that hugged Melech's underside and clasped together above him like a collapsed hammock. The poor creature swung helplessly and was turning in a slow twirl. Landon flinched—twice—when it appeared Melech was about to bump against the ship. Soon, however, they had him hanging in the open air higher than the railing. *Now what?* Landon wondered. They weren't going to just leave him hanging out there, were they?

Melech looked down at him. "It's good to see you again, young Landon."

Landon smiled at his friend's glossy black eyes. "Hey, Melech. It's good to see you, too."

Somehow, the men managed to swing the pulley system around. Before Landon realized what was happening, Melech was flying at him like a carousel horse gone out of control.

"Whoa!" Landon scampered backward. He lost control himself and fell hard to the deck. His telescope clattered and began to roll.

Melech was now hanging over the deck, his hooves about four feet above it. He hovered only for an instant before the taut ropes loosened and dropped him to the planks. As the deck shuddered from the impact, Landon remembered another time Melech had crashed to the ground. That time, Landon had been on top of the horse, and they had plummeted all the way to earth from a giant chessboard in the sky.

Grabbing the telescope mid-roll and jumping up, Landon said, "Welcome aboard! Boy, it's good to see you." He patted Melech's thick neck and clasped his mane between his fingers.

Melech almost purred, ending in a staccato whinny.

Hardy appeared over the railing and clambered aboard. He was wearing a brown vest and a brown hat. He strode right over to Landon. Something was strapped onto his back, and Landon noticed the other two fellows had similar packs.

Hardy flashed a big grin, his teeth pointing in all directions. "Hey-ho, Landon Snow."

"Hey. . .ho. . .Hardy." Landon was about to extend his hand, trying to remember if he had ever shaken Hardy's hand before or if shaking hands was even a custom in Wonderwood. But Hardy had turned to face Holly and Bridget, who were standing off to the side, watching. Epops was perched on Bridget's shoulder, playfully poking at one of her curls.

"Hey-ho, Holly." Hardy doffed his hat and bowed. "Hidy-ho, little miss." He glanced up at Bridget from his bowed position. Bridget giggled and waved.

Hardy pointed to the other two men. "Wagglewhop, Battleroot, say hey to de little ladies."

They exchanged self-conscious waves, and Wagglewhop—in the black vest and red hat—grunted while Battleroot—red vest and black hat—had a brief sneezing fit as if he were allergic to little girls.

Well, Landon had guessed half right on their names. Though he was sure it was pronounced Waggle*whip*, not *whop*. He still wanted to call these fellows Odds, as that's what they had been when he'd first encountered their kind. A thought struck him. *These fellows tried to take Melech away from me before. And they even shot arrows at us—and at Hardy. Can they be trusted? What are they doing here?*

Of course, everything and everyone in Wonderwood had changed once the giant gold coin had been melted and they had driven out Malus Quidam's evil shadows. *So they're not Odds anymore,* Landon reminded himself. *They're just regular valley folk.*

Whatever that meant. Battleroot's and Wagglewhip's features—like Hardy's—reminded Landon of elves or dwarves or some such creatures. They weren't exactly like human beings.

Hardy recapped his messy mop and swung back toward Landon. "Ludo teach me to do de bowdy and howdy and dem good manners." His teeth appeared, an orthodontist's dream job—or nightmare—and Hardy gave Landon his signature wink. But then Hardy's expression changed to serious.

Hardy took a step closer. "You have any of dem dreams or sightseeings, you know?" He raised his eyebrows, pushing up his brown, three-cornered hat. Landon almost wanted to laugh, but something in Hardy's eyes kept his smile in check.

"Sightseeing?" Landon raised his own eyebrows. Then he frowned. "Well, we've mostly seen this." He gestured with his hand to indicate the sea. "And we saw a mystery ship following us last night, but it turns out it was you." He glanced over at the ark. Noah—er, Vates had disappeared from the deck. Landon wanted to ask if *she* was aboard, and now he wondered about Ludo, too—with somewhat mixed feelings—but the moment didn't seem right for it.

Something thumped and bumped down below. Hardy swung around and issued a command. "De jolly boat! Hoist it high. Hidy ho!"

Wagglewhip and Battleroot sprang into action. Within minutes, they had the large rowboat up and over the rail. It remained hanging under the pulleys over the deck, but they secured it so that it wouldn't swing.

Hardy removed his hat and scratched his head. When he looked at Landon again, he appeared anxious. His forehead was more wrinkled than Landon had ever seen it. Hardy frowned. "Vates dot. . . ." He paused and sighed. "Vates was sure you would see. . .would see *some*ding."

"Vates thought I would see something." Landon rubbed the back of his neck. What was it he was supposed to have seen? "Well," he said finally, "I did have a dream last night. Melech and I were on the chessboard being chased, but at first it was two ships. It was the ark chasing this ship, I think. Although last night I didn't know it was an ark."

Could this be the vision Vates was looking for? It seemed doubtful.

Hardy's eyes had widened with hope. Then the light faded from them, and he sagged his shoulders. "Hmm. Dat dream doesn't sound right. It's from de past. Looking for someding else. Someding in de future." He sighed. "Harrumph."

Landon felt like apologizing, although he didn't know for what. Melech scraped the deck with his hoof. He thrust out his muzzle. "Vates thought you might see a dream or vision that would aid in our quest. Without your help, young Landon, this journey may prove useless for all of us."

Landon fell quiet for a minute. A dream or a *vision.* Something stirred inside him, but for the moment his mind was blank and confused. "Quest? What quest?"

Hardy went to the railing to gaze at the ark. Epops fluttered to the railing and hopped close to Hardy as if to console him. Wagglewhip sighed and grunted. Battleroot sneezed and then gazed up at the droopy sails, snuffling.

Melech explained. "We are headed to an island. Ludo knows the way to the island, and Wagglewhip knows the way into the island. That is, to a dark and secret place on the island." The horse made a throat-clearing noise.

Landon frowned. If anything, he felt even more confused and lost. An island? A dark and secret place? What was Melech talking about?

A breeze flowed through from nowhere. It wasn't much, but after floating dead in the water for so long, any air movement felt refreshing. The ship started to rock with more force. Even the sails perked up. A moment later, as Landon looked hopefully at the sheets, they fell limp again.

"Are we going to Hawaii?" Bridget asked. "That's an island. And are we going into a volcano? I mean, an empty one? That would be dark and secret."

Everyone looked at her. Hardy said, "A-why?" Presumably he meant Hawaii. Hardy shook his head. "No A-why, and no fall-cano." Hardy turned away from Bridget and grazed the others in turn with his eyes. Something almost wild filled his look. It was a little disturbing. When his gaze met Landon's, Hardy paused. "Arcanum," he said in a loud whisper.

Landon felt his back stiffen. "Arcanum?"

Another breeze ruffled the sails. The wind was definitely picking up. A gust shoved the ship ahead like a giant hand pushing a toy boat through the water. Then it let up, and they were drifting and rocking again.

The sudden pitch had caused Landon to stumble backward and then fall forward, catching himself on his knees. Now as the ship gently swayed, he held this position. Something was stirring inside him again. *What is it?* His right hand held the telescope against his leg. His left hand lightly clutched his lower thigh. He closed his eyes, and the deck became a field. *A football field. Of course!*

The vision seemed to fall right into place. It felt obvious now, as it had been there all along. But there had been many distractions for Landon and his sisters in the meantime.

Blue twenty-two, blue twenty-two. Hut. . .hut—hut-hut!

Landon lurched forward, opening his eyes. Melech was watching him.

"I saw animals," said Landon.

"Well, there is the bird and myself," said Melech evenly.

But Hardy was turning from the railing, his eyes bugging. "Aminals?"

Landon nodded. "Yeah."

Holly stepped in excitedly. "That's right. At the football game! You said you saw animals instead of players."

The ship leaned back, and Landon tilted forward to balance himself against the rising angle. Everyone was leaning.

"What animals?" said Bridget. "What football game? What's happening to the ship?"

The ship slowly came back down but then continued pitching forward. Everyone leaned back.

Landon looked at Hardy, sensing something. Wagglewhip and Battleroot had moved closer, too, but then stopped as the deck slanted backward. "I saw animals in a vision."

A blob of drool fell from Hardy's gaping jaw like a yo-yo on a string. Then it broke and fell to the deck. Hardy licked his lips.

"Den it must be true, what Vates said." Hardy grinned, and he was his old cheerful self again.

"Vates?" said Bridget. "What did he say?"

With each tilt of the ship, the group was somehow gathering closer together. Now they were practically in a huddle—Hardy, Wagglewhip, Battleroot, Holly, Bridget with Epops on her shoulder again, Landon, and Melech.

Landon felt a tingly finger climb his spine and tickle his brain. "Yes, what did he say, Hardy? What did Vates say?"

Hardy would have made a funny-looking quarterback. But right now, it felt like he was calling the play. His brown hat had slid back, revealing neat, angled eyebrows that appeared out of place on his otherwise soft and rather sloppy-appearing body. He licked his lips again, eagerly eyeing each one in their tight little circle.

"Vates say, 'It's time to get de aminals and bring dem back to Wonderwood.' "

As soon as Hardy shared Vates' announcement about getting the animals, the ship seemed to pick itself right up into the air. Landon and his friends felt momentarily suspended before suddenly charging toward the front of the ship like football players breaking from a huddle. Their circle broke apart, and a few of them fell to the deck. Landon dropped his telescope, sending it rolling to Holly, who scooped it up. Just like that, the ship was sailing at top speed. Waves swooshed below and splashed over the front railing. Salty spray rained on everything. The sails billowed overhead, taut as balloons.

"Go tell Vates!" Hardy hollered. He waved his arms at Bridget. Then Landon noticed Epops scrunched down on Bridget's shoulder. Hardy pointed at the bird and then flung his arm away.

"Tell him! De boy has seen a vision. He's seen de aminals!"

Epops squatted like a ball of feathers. The bird seemed to want to stay and play with Bridget.

"Giddah, birdie. Giddah!"

After more frantic waving, Epops finally burst into the air as if launched from a slingshot. He swooped over the sails and circled the crow's nest before flying across the water in a rhythmic rising and falling motion. The bird's call faded into the wind.

"Twee-too! Twee-too! Twee. . ."

"Hey, Landon, check this out." Holly stood along the curved rail near the front of the ship. She was looking through the telescope.

As soon as Landon reached the rail, he gasped. The water hissed below them in a white fury, breaking away and trailing behind. They were tearing the sea apart with this ship.

"Look," said Holly, handing him the scope.

Landon had barely caught his breath before he gasped again. He grabbed the rail as the ship crashed into the sea, rose high, and then crashed again. His hair was dripping. Tasting brine on his lips, he peered through the scope. "They're keeping up with us," he declared loudly in amazement.

"Yeah, check out how." Holly was practically shouting.

At first, he didn't see it. Then Landon noticed a huge, long beam sticking out from the side of the ark, dragging a large black net. No, it wasn't dragging the net; the net was dragging the ark!

"They've got a sail sticking out," said Landon, realizing that's what it was, not a net.

"Pretty weird, huh?"

"Yeah!" Landon was shouting himself. "It looks like a batwing!"

He felt a tap on his shoulder. Landon lowered the scope

and looked at Hardy. Wagglewhip and Battleroot stood behind him. They looked excited—who wouldn't be excited by this instant race at sea? But there was something else, too. The one in the black vest, Wagglewhip, looked especially concerned.

"Need to talk," Hardy hollered.

Landon nodded, feeling wonderfully like a real sea captain being summoned by his first mate and two crew members. He handed the telescope back to Holly. "Keep a lookout," he commanded, "for an island."

"Aye-aye," Holly shouted. "I wish I had a raincoat!"

Landon grinned as he followed the three fellows toward the back of the ship. The rocking was definitely more exaggerated in the front. The movement at the middle of the ship, by comparison, felt fairly gentle. With Epops gone, Bridget was now standing alongside Melech, holding one of his legs like a tree. Melech didn't seem to mind.

Hardy and the others paused at the door, and Landon entered first. As soon as they were inside the captain's cabin, Battleroot let out three sneezes in rapid succession. Maybe it was the sea he was allergic to. Hardy went around the desk to the wide window, taking in the retreating sea. The other two stood off to the side, wringing out their hats. They held them limply and looked sadly at Landon.

"Me most humblest apologies for behaviors past," said Wagglewhip gravely. "We were not ourselves for a long time. We'd like to blame the shadows. . . ." He hung his head. "But we all gave in to the lures and the shines of the Coin."

The ship still rolled with great forward momentum. But it seemed much quieter and more peaceful in here with the sun and spray and noise shut out. Wagglewhip was sighing—was he sniffling? And Battleroot kept glancing at Landon and twitching his nose. When Landon looked at him, the poor fellow stared decidedly at the floor. Speaking of the floor, something was rolling around on it, thumping here and there. Eventually, a battered orange came into view.

Landon cleared his throat. He hadn't felt so awkward in a long time. It was almost as difficult to acknowledge an apology as it was to dish one out.

"That was a long time ago," said Landon. "And, well, I forgive you."

The words seemed to release him as well as the valley men. They stood up straighter, and when Battleroot sneezed into his hat, he came out from behind it with a big grin on his face. His eyes were watering from the sneeze, or from the forgiveness—or both.

Hardy turned from the window. Standing behind the desk with his hands clasped behind his back, he looked as if he belonged in the captain's cabin. Boy, what a change from when Landon had first seen him near the Echoing Green, when Ludo ran the place and "Tardy Hardy," as he'd been called, seemed to be the least of all the valley folk, who were called "Odds" back then.

"Dey already sorried to me and Melech, and Ditty and Vates, even dough *dey* never got shot at by arrows." Hardy stretched out an arm to reveal a scar. He looked at it proudly. "Helped make me tough."

Wagglewhip and Battleroot flinched slightly and looked away. They seemed not to want to be reminded of wounds they may have caused.

"Ludo sorried, too. Sometimes too much. Don't dink he'll be better till we get de aminals back. He feels baddest about de empty forest now."

Landon tried to put things together. He remembered Ditty saying that Ludo had loved animals and cared for them. . .before the first Descent. Then Malus Quidam's shadows had come down, and Ludo had changed from being quiet and kind to being pushy and mean. Instead of caring for the animals, he had them all taken away—apparently banished to this island.

All except for the fireflies, who fell asleep, and one tiny bird named Epops, who was found by Vates.

Thinking of Ludo and looking at these two fellows who had once inspired fear, Landon now felt only pity. Any lingering resentment or suspicion was behind them like the sea behind the ship.

"Is Ditty on the ark?"

The question popped out seemingly on its own, though it had been simmering in Landon's mind since he'd first seen Epops and recognized Vates.

The three stout men looked at him. Landon waited for them to grin or chide him or wink, but they only looked.

"Aye," Battleroot said in a gruff, wheezy voice. "Aye. . *.Aye. . . Aye-choo!*" He blew his plump red nose into his soppy black hat. "She is."

It was all Landon could do to contain himself. He wanted to jump up and down or holler or run around the deck. Instead, he slowly nodded.

Hardy leaned onto the desk. "Dere's someding you should know, Landon."

Landon felt a catch in his throat. "What is that?"

"Ditty's mum and dad. . .dey. . ."

Wagglewhip and Battleroot were wringing their hats again, though no more water was dripping out.

Landon's heart was feeling heavy. "What is it? What about her parents?" He was astounded to even hear of them. He had never considered her having a mother and father, strange as that thought seemed now.

Hardy sighed. "Well, we don't know. . . . But dey might be on de island, too, wid de aminals."

Landon's heart began to pound. "So we could find her parents?"

Hardy looked up. "She doesn't know. And we don't want to—" Hardy's lip had begun to tremble.

Landon felt hot jabs of water around his own eyes, and he fought to hold them back. "Get her hopes up," he said, finishing Hardy's sentence. "We don't want to get her hopes up, because. . ."

Now it was Hardy's turn. After another sigh, he said, "Dey might be dead. Or worse dan dat."

Landon was frowning so hard that his face hurt. Worse than dead? What could be worse than that? The pounding of his heart felt like a hammer beating stone. Landon's own lip was quivering. "What do you mean?" he said. "What could be. . .worse?"

Hardy leaned on the desk, but he lifted his gaze toward Wagglewhip.

Wagglewhip knows the way into *the island. . . .to a dark and secret place.*

What was it Wagglewhip knew?

Wagglewhip straightened and took a deep breath. He stopped twisting his hat. His eyes slowly met Landon's.

"They went with the animals; we think hoping to bring them back to the valley." He had to clear his throat. "Ditty's mum and dad did not give in to the shadows. But when they got to the island. . ."

Wagglewhip's voice wavered, and his eyes fell. Landon waited.

"When they got to the island," he continued, "they encountered something greater—well, worse than the shadows. The shadows could only whisper to you until you listened to them, and then they could direct you according to Malus Quidam's will. But the Arcans are like living shadows. They're real." He patted his thick hands together around the hat. "They're like us but not like us."

"What Wagglewhip is saying," said Hardy, "is dat Arcans don't whisper and tempt; dey draw blood. And dey're like us because dey have bodies. But dey're not like us because dey can't be turned back to good. Dere's no good for dem to turn back to. Dey've always been bad."

One of Wagglewhip's legs had started shaking. He appeared to be trying to control it, but it kept jiggling nonetheless. Landon was starting to feel a little nervous.

"Show him," said Hardy.

With his leg still shaking, Wagglewhip rolled back one of his sleeves and turned his arm over. Landon took a step closer. Whereas Hardy's scar was a simple stripe from the graze of an arrow, this scar was more like a tattoo. Landon felt his own knees grow weak as he looked at it. Emblazoned into Wagglewhip's tough flesh was an X with the number 8 over it. Except the X was comprised of two crossed bones, and the 8 had two dots in the top half for eyes. It wasn't a number; it was a skull.

Dizziness began to overtake him, and Landon felt like crawling into the bed. He forced himself to concentrate. And to breathe.

"What could be worse than death?" Landon asked. He was pondering the question himself as much as seeking an answer from his friends.

"Living on the Island of Arcanum. . .forever." Wagglewhip said this bluntly, and finally, his leg stopped shaking.

Landon swallowed hard. It felt like the orange that had been rolling around the floor was now lodged in his throat. "So. . .you're actually hoping they might be dead?" It sounded like the worst question one could ask.

Battleroot let out a sob and then a sneeze, followed by a trumpeting snort into his hat.

"We don't know if we even want to know," Hardy said plainly.

Landon walked to the bed now, where he sat down. This was almost too much to absorb. "Ditty never said anything about a mom or dad."

Hardy turned back to the window. The light was dimming slightly, the colors of the sky and the sea shifting toward darker hues. Landon caught a glimpse through the angled window past Hardy. The horizon went up, and then it went down. The outside motion seemed like nothing compared to the emotional reeling Landon was experiencing inside his heart and mind.

"No," said Hardy. "Vates dinks she might have forgotten about dem—on purpose."

"On purpose," Landon said dully. How could you ever forget your parents? Then again, if the pain was too much to bear. . .

"What about the animals?" said Landon. "Are they suffering

'worse than death,' too?"

Wagglewhip spun around, apparently happy to change the subject from Ditty's parents. "No," he said brightly, considering the circumstances. "Animals are different from us—and from them—too. They can suffer here"—he pinched the skin above his tattoo and winced—"but not the same here or here." Wagglewhip pointed at his head and then at his heart.

Landon nodded, thinking he understood.

"So," Wagglewhip continued, "animals aren't as much. . . fun. . .to torture."

Landon flinched. Any excitement he'd had about seeing this island was gone. Replaced by dread. And fear.

"You're the only one who's seen them?" Landon asked.

Wagglewhip nodded. "Them—and their chief. Chief Arcanum."

"How did you get away?" said Landon, a flame of suspicion rekindling.

Wagglewhip showed him his arm and pointed to the nasty purplish skull and crossbones. "Signed a deal. I agreed to serve the shadows and keep all the animals out of Wonderwood."

Landon nodded, regretting his suspicion. He remembered now, way back, overhearing Ludo speaking with another Odd about taking Melech away. *That was you,* Landon thought. He shuddered at the idea of Melech being taken to this island as a captive. And now, here was Wagglewhip returning, ready to try to get the animals back again.

"The Arcans aren't going to be very happy to see you, are they, Wagglewhip?" Landon asked.

Wagglewhip grinned mischievously. A twinkle shone in his eyes. "No, I don't think so, young Landon."

"So how are we supposed to do this?" said Landon. This quest was sounding thornier by the moment. Would it even be possible? "Why did Vates want to know if I had a vision? I saw some animals on a football field, but I still don't know what it means."

Hardy came around the desk and strode into the cubbyhole. He came out with four oranges and lobbed one to each person. Hardy tossed his orange and caught it a few times before taking a big bite from it, orange peel and all. Chomping the fruit and dripping juice and pulp, Hardy gulped and then grinned.

"You know what Vates would say your vision means, Landon Snow?"

Landon found himself leaning on the edge of the bed. It almost felt like the old prophet was here with them rather than across the water on the ark. "What does it mean?" Landon asked. He could see Vates' eyes looking at him and hear Vates' voice speaking in response.

"It means de Auctor has a plan."

Well, it almost sounded like Vates' voice.

After they each downed another orange and some bread and drank a mug of ginger ale, Landon and Hardy brought some grub out to Melech and to Landon's sisters. Wagglewhip and Battleroot followed with the jugs. The food and drink didn't taste too great anymore, as Holly had stated earlier. But they provided needed nourishment. After a couple of good belches, Landon felt even better. He gazed across the expanse of open water to the ark. As light drained from the sky, the ark became a silhouette. At least now Landon knew who was on board.

Vates, Ludo, Ditty. . .

Tonight he needn't worry over who—or what—was chasing them. Tonight he would be considering something more frightening: the island that lay ahead. Landon was convinced the Arcans were thoroughly evil, though he realized he still didn't know what they were actually capable of doing. Or what they looked like.

"Twee-too! Twee-too!"

"Epops!"

The bird had returned undetected, and Bridget was the first to respond. Epops swooped right in to perch on Bridget's shoulder. Then the bird hopped into the air and hovered like a fluffy hummingbird, its beak pointing back toward the ark.

"De ark is turning," said Hardy, an edge to his voice. "How do we steer dis ship?" He raised his hands and shrugged. "We need to follow dem. Ludo knows de way."

"Holly," said Landon. "Can you take Wagglewhip and Battleroot to the helm and show them—"

"How to turn the pages?" Holly flashed her brother a grin. Strips of blond hair lay plastered across her face. She didn't seem to mind, although she did seem to detect something serious in the air. Her grin vanished. "Is something wrong?"

Landon glanced at Bridget, then back at Holly. He sighed. "Show them how to—turn the pages." He tried to smile, and the effort felt strained. "I'll talk to you later."

"Yes, sir," said Holly. Then to Wagglewhip and Battleroot, "Right this way, gentlemen. To the bridge."

Before marching off, she handed Landon the telescope. "The sky's not as red tonight," she said. "No sailors' delight, I guess."

"Ah, you're not superstitious, are you?" he kidded. But it felt flat. "No, things aren't looking as good tonight," he said. Holly gave him a lingering look, but Landon motioned for her to go on. "Later," he said.

Holly headed off with her crew.

"Are we going to stay out here another night, Landon?" asked Bridget.

Landon put his arm around her. "I think so. Is that okay?"

Bridget looked at Melech and then at Epops, who had

returned to her shoulder. She nodded. "Yeah. I guess so. And Landon?"

"Yes?"

"Is the island really safe to go to, do you think?"

Was Bridget a mind reader, too? Landon couldn't lie, not about this. "I think you might have to stay on the ship," he said. He could never forgive himself if something happened to Bridget. "Somebody will stay with you."

"Who? Holly? Or Melech?" She hugged the horse's leg, and he whinnied.

"I—I don't know. Probably Vates, and maybe Ditty." Landon gazed at the dark outline of the ark, which was now pulling ahead of them and to the right. A sharp yearning jabbed his chest.

"Oh, and maybe Ludo, too," Landon added. "I think Ludo will definitely be staying with the ship."

"Lu—*who*?" Bridget's voice rose in concern. "You're not all going to leave me, are you?"

"No," said Landon crouching down to her level. "No, Bridget. We're not going to leave you. But when we get to the island, well, you're going to have to be brave and wait for us. Okay?"

Bridget's eyes gleamed, and her cheeks puffed out. Eventually, she nodded.

"Okay," said Landon. "Now, before it's too dark, I need to go up for a better look."

"Up where?"

Landon gazed up at the crow's nest. Stars were peeking down through ragged clouds beyond the masts and sails. "Up there."

"Oh."

"How 'bout if you take Melech and Epops inside the cabin. You know where you slept last night? And maybe see if you could find any more clothes in there. You don't have to look anywhere else though, okay?"

"Okay," said Bridget.

The air was getting chill, and she was soaked through. The poor thing. Landon looked at his own shirt and pulled it away from his skin. The wet fabric made a sucking sound before he let it smack back. Goodness. No wonder it felt chillier tonight.

"Bridget," he called after her. She and Melech stopped and looked back. "We all need dry clothes tonight. See what you can find. Holler up to Holly if you need help, okay?"

Bridget gave him a thumbs-up and continued climbing and descending the rising and falling deck.

After watching her and Melech go, Landon puffed out his cheeks and blew out a stream of air.

"Quite de challenge, eh?" said Hardy. "Watching out for your sisters and commanding a ship and planning to get de aminals back. Whew-whee. Yessirree."

Landon was shivering, but he almost laughed. "Yeah," he said. "And I'm only twelve years old!"

"How 'bout I climb up dere, and you can go help de little miss and get dried up and all dat, eh?" Hardy held out his hand.

"Do you need some dry clothes, too?" asked Landon.

"Got 'em in my pack. Plus dis skin doesn't get so twitchery as yours." Hardy pushed up both his sleeves and slapped his arms. "Ahhh!" he said, acting as if the cold air was just what he needed.

Landon smiled, and his teeth chattered. "Oh–ho–ho–kay."

He gave Hardy the telescope and headed for the cabin. Turning back as Hardy was beginning to scramble up the rope ladder, Landon yelled, "Thanks, Hardy!"

"Welcomes, welcomes," returned a voice from beyond the sails.

The captain's cabin was dark. Before Landon could say his youngest sister's name, however, she flicked a match and touched it to a lantern wick. When Landon saw Bridget's face in the glow, he felt a smile push at his cheeks. He had two wonderful, resourceful sisters, didn't he? Sure they could nitpick each other at times and get on each other's nerves. But when push came to shove, they came together and took care of each other.

Their parents would be proud of them.

Landon thought about Ditty's missing parents. He couldn't imagine being in such a situation—not having his parents around and not even knowing what had happened to them. He couldn't help hoping that Ditty's mom and dad were still alive. And that they would find them and bring them back.

But what if they weren't alive? Well, then Ditty would probably never learn their fate. Unless they came across two skeletons that they somehow knew were—

No. Landon shook his head. He could not accept this thought.

What if they were alive but were somehow. . .changed?

The questions were impossible to answer, so Landon tried not to think about them. He was, however, thinking about the animals. Specifically, he was replaying the scene at the football game over and over in his mind. There were five bears, he was quite sure—*the offensive linemen*—and then a panther and a dark wolf—*defensive tacklers. They were attackers.* Then there was the ref who looked like a zebra, and his coach who had behaved like a gorilla, but only for a moment.

Had there been any other animals?

Yes. When Landon was lying on the ground, he had laughed. . . .

Like a hyena.

And one more thing. . .

The football. It had become some sort of animal, too. Landon never had figured out what it was. Only that it was rather light and springy and furry. He'd been holding it in his arms, and then, when the wolf stood over him, he had flung the furry creature away. The next thing he knew, it was a football again, sitting on the grass.

Something coarse and dry was thrust against his belly. "Here. It's the best I could find."

Landon looked down to see Bridget holding a stack of stiff, folded material. He took it and studied it. "Is this a uniform?"

"Well, they're clothes, I think," said Bridget. "Mine has sleeves and legs, though they're a little long. And they're kind of hard and scratchy."

Bridget's hair had been drawn back, and she was in a new set of clothes. Or a very old set of clothes, more likely. She looked like a miniature sailor or soldier out of a history book. Landon tried not to laugh.

"Where did you change?" he asked. Scratchy or not, these clothes were dry.

"Right over there in that funny little room. That's where the clothes are, too."

Bridget pointed to a doorway opposite the food pantry from the entryway. Landon stepped over to it and peered inside, allowing lantern light to enter from behind him. The door had no latch or knob; it was simply a section of paneling that slid over to reveal the room. Shelves lined either side, stacked with more uniforms. The bottom shelf on the left held a row of boots. *Those might come in handy on the island*, Landon thought, wiggling his toes inside his wet, squishy shoes. He stepped inside, cautiously standing, as the space was barely taller than him. It was more of a crawlspace than a room.

"Did you close the door to change?" said Landon.

"Of course," said Bridget.

Landon held out the shirt and then the trousers or knickers or whatever you called these sorts of pants. Once he was confident he would know what to do in the dark, Landon slid the door shut and changed into his new uniform.

After changing into dry clothes (which included dry underclothes, if one really must know), Landon wasn't too keen on putting his wet, squishy shoes back on. He found some rough socks, which softened some once they were stretched over his feet, and also a pair of boots. The boots would need some breaking in.

Within the cramped closet, Landon discovered another sliding door leading to yet another closet. In this second closet were hanging blue uniform coats as well as belts and some other sorts of straps. One belt with a fancy silver clasp had a long strip hanging from it. It was actually a long pocket or case for a sword. A *scabbard.* Landon felt like a cunning warrior as he strapped it around his waist. The sheath would keep the sword from accidentally nicking his leg. It would also keep the sword from clanging, should it bump against something hard.

Of course, these thoughts seemed fairly absurd. Landon didn't consider actually putting a sword in the scabbard and carrying it about. When he stepped out from the closet, Hardy was waiting for him.

"Did you see anything from the crow's nest?" asked Landon.

Hardy was eyeing Landon's new outfit up and down. On the second pass, his eyes stopped on the belt and the scabbard.

"What's dat?" Hardy pointed.

"Oh," Landon said, feeling a bit silly and wanting to take it off, "it's for carrying a sword. But we're not going to actually—"

Landon paused, watching Hardy.

Hardy had looked up. His face appeared a shadowy mask in the dim lantern light. But something else shimmered in his eyes. He was breathing heavily, and not from his quick scamper up and down from the crow's nest. When he spoke, a slight tremor rattled his voice. Landon had never seen or heard Hardy this way. His stout, jovial friend seemed almost. . .afraid.

"Are dere more of dose?"

Landon nodded. "There's a whole 'nother closet in there with belts and things."

Hardy swallowed. "And are dere. . .swords on dis ship?"

Again Landon nodded, more slowly this time. He was sensing fear. He was also sensing—something else. A boldness and determination was taking shape in Hardy as Landon had never seen. Even when they'd planned to attack Malus Quidam's shadows at the Echoing Green, Hardy hadn't seemed daunted or fazed. Now he seemed daunted but also more daring.

"Show me," said Hardy.

Landon nodded and went to light another lantern. Then he turned to lead Hardy down to the weapons deck.

"Where are you going?" said Bridget from the bed.

Landon had thought she'd fallen asleep, but apparently she'd only been lying there resting. And listening.

"Down below decks." Landon was aware that he was talking sort of strange. But the language seemed to fit. Seeing his little sister sitting up, Landon added, "You can stay here, Bridget. With Melech and Epops."

"Okay." She laid back down.

Melech had been looking out the window. Upon hearing his name, however, he perked up and stepped over to the bed. *Clomp de-clomp clomp.* Epops was perched on a lantern handle, swaying against the leaning of the ship.

"Come on," said Landon. With each descending step, he could feel his heart beating louder and faster.

When they reached the cannon room, Hardy gasped and then said, "Dunder guns."

"Dunder guns?" said Landon.

"Dunder—*boom, boom*—dunder guns." Hardy flashed out his fingers with each *boom.*

"Oh, *thunder* guns. *Boom, boom.* We call them cannons."

When Hardy picked up a sword and tossed it easily from one hand to the other, swishing it neatly through the air as if he were drawing tiny letters with its point, Landon sucked in his breath and held it. Like Bartholomew G. Benneford, there also seemed to be more to Hardy's history than Landon knew. Had Hardy been a soldier—or a sailor—too? Or perhaps. . .a pirate?

"Where did you learn to do that?" asked Landon. He was transfixed.

Hardy stopped, holding the sword straight out as an extension of his arm. An arm, Landon noticed with great admiration, that didn't even quiver.

"I was trained as a little boy. Never fought. Only train. Until de first Descent. Den our tools—and armor and swords—taken away. Tools were hidden around de Echoing Green. Armor and swords—never seen dem again."

"Who took dem? I mean, them?" Landon felt his face grow warm.

Hardy slid the sword into the rack. "Dey were sent wid de aminals. To de island." He turned and looked at Landon.

"The Arcans," said Landon. "They have all your weapons."

Hardy nodded. "Dey have dese, too, I dink." He gestured toward the cannons.

And we're supposed to waltz in there and take the animals back? Landon thought. But aloud he said, "What do they need all those weapons for, with only animals around?"

Hardy shrugged. "Who know? I dink dey just didn't want *us* to have dem. Dey're probably all sitting in a big junk pile or burned for scrap." He shrugged again.

"How do you know they have thunder cannons?" *Thunder cannons.* Landon smiled. Hardy's language was catching.

"Vates told me about dem. I never seen one before until now. Vates say dey can shoot dings from deir ships, dings much worse dan arrows."

"Vates. . . ," Landon said. But then he decided not to ask. Vates just seemed to know a lot about a lot of things.

When they headed back up, they were caught by Holly's voice from the bridge. "You're wearing different clothes!" she hollered.

Landon looked up. His mind had been so busy the past hour, he'd forgotten about Holly still being in her wet clothes. "I'm sor—" Landon started but then stopped. Holly was wearing a stiff uniform, too. "Hey!" Landon's tone changed to mock annoyance. "Where'd you get that nice outfit?"

"Same place as you, I guess. A little bird told me about it."

Epops swooped out of nowhere, and both Landon and Hardy ducked, covering their heads. Thunder guns and swords and fighting were in the backs of their minds now. They weren't about to stand and wait for an object to hit them.

The bird rose to the bridge, fluttered around Holly and the two new helmsmen, and then came down to alight on Landon's shoulder. He stood, smiling.

"You scared me, little bird."

Epops tilted his head. "Twee-too."

They walked inside the captain's quarters to find Bridget softly snoring, one little hand stretched out from the bed to touch Melech's front leg. Melech's head was bowed low toward her. It sounded like he was asleep, too.

"I can't imagine sleeping like that," whispered Landon. "Standing up." He shook his head.

"You should probably sleep somehow, dough," said Hardy. "We need to rest for tomorrow."

Landon looked at Hardy, knowing he was right. The thought of tromping through a mysterious island in this stiff, scratchy uniform sounded exhausting enough. The thought of facing Arcans—well, that wasn't something he wanted to think about anymore tonight. Another thought did strike Landon, however.

He tapped Hardy's shoulder as Hardy gazed distractedly out the window. "Hey, did you see anything from the crow's nest? You never told me."

Hardy didn't move. He kept staring out the window at the darkly shimmering sea. Finally, he sighed. "I saw it," he whispered simply.

Landon caught his breath. He leaned closer. "You saw it? You saw the island?" He could hardly keep his voice down.

Hardy gave the faintest of nods. "We're circling it. Good night."

Landon had a hard time falling asleep. *We're circling the island, the Island of Arcanum.* Even had he not known about the animals from Wonderwood being there or the evil-sounding Arcans, he still would have kept dwelling on it. Wondering what the place looked like. Excited to explore it. Yet fearful, too.

Then he thought of the possibility of finding Ditty's parents. . . .

But was that really possible? Could they really be there?

Go to sleep. You need to get some rest.

Yeah, right. Sure, I can sleep now. Now that we're circling the island.

Had Holly seen the island? She hadn't let on if she had. Apparently, she had come down to the captain's cabin, changed clothes, and gone back up to the bridge. She hadn't stayed on the bridge for too long, though. Soon after Hardy had told him to get some sleep, Holly returned and slipped into the bed next to

Bridget—where Landon had tried to rest briefly. Holly was tired, too. She laid down and was quiet.

Landon slipped outside, where it was too dark to see anything, he decided. *Unless you were up in the crow's nest.* Holly hadn't seen it. Only Hardy had. They were probably circling beyond the range of normal eyesight.

But what if the islanders could see them? Landon shuddered at the thought of mysterious men on the island peering out at them.

Landon found his bed of folded netting and laid down. *It's time to ask for help.* Tired as he was, he couldn't close his eyes quite yet. The clouds suddenly seemed to spread just for him, and the stars pulsed a soothing rhythm. *I know you're with me,* Landon said to the Auctor. *I know you're with us. I do. I do.*

As Landon's eyes drooped, he began seeing something in the stars.

From Orion's Belt, he plucked a large sword. Wielding it with one hand like a skilled warrior, he pointed the sword at the stars of other constellations. With each touch, his sword grew brighter and felt lighter, while the stars lost none of their force for the giving. Finally, Landon brought the sword down by his side. It had become heavy again, and the weight of it felt good, drawing him down to a place of rest.

Landon awoke to shouting.

"Land ho! Land ho!"

Was someone calling his name? No, it didn't sound quite right. The snap of sails and the salty sea air reminded him where he was.

"Off the port bow, ho!"

Feeling the rocking of the ship, Landon remembered something else.

The island!

When he got up from the net, his back wasn't as stiff as it had been the day before. Besides gaining sea legs, Landon's whole body was adjusting. Toughening up. He checked for his telescope, but before reaching the ship's railing, he realized he didn't need it.

The island.

It rose before them and a little to their left in the early daylight. It was merely a dark shape—a mass upon the water. When Landon brought up his telescope, however, he could make out jagged outcroppings of rock and something that looked like smoke rising from the center of the island. Apparently Hardy was wrong when he'd said there was no "fallcano." The entire island looked like a smoking volcano.

Landon swallowed. Any curiosity and desire he'd had to explore the island was quickly vanishing. The closer the island came, the more Landon wanted to turn and sail away from it.

The animals are there, he reminded himself.

And maybe Ditty's parents.

He took a deep breath. *We have to go in. The Auctor has a plan.*

"Top o' de morning, Landon."

Hardy stood next to him and leaned on the railing. The appearance of his friend made Landon feel better. At least he wasn't going on this mission alone.

"Good morning," said Landon, trying to sound cheerful.

"I thought you said there wasn't a volcano on the island."

Hardy gazed across the water. The sea gently rose and fell, whooshing against the ship and then swishing away. "No fall-cano. At least not active for a long time."

Landon frowned. "But there's smoke coming up from it. Look." Hardy had to see the smoke. Was it possible they were headed toward the wrong island?

Hardy's expression remained fixed. "Not smoke," he said. "Shadows."

"Wha—" Landon checked himself and looked, peering through the telescope. "But how can there be. . . ?" What he saw through the lens made his blood freeze. "Oh no. . . ."

The island was getting closer. The "smoke" was indeed too dark and black to be smoke. It didn't simply float up from the rock and dissipate into the sky. It circled like a funnel or a black tornado.

"Oh no," Landon said again. His stomach felt like it was on the deck with his feet. He lowered the telescope, relieved to let the island fall back into the distance. Landon knew without asking, but he had to say it anyway. "Is it Malus Quidam?"

"Aye," said Hardy.

"But I thought we defeated him on the Echoing Green? How did he come back? And how did he get here?"

Landon wished Vates were here to answer his questions and hopefully offer some comfort. Then again, Hardy seemed to be becoming more like Vates all the time. Or at least Hardy was picking up some of the old man's knowledge and sense of things.

"We did beat him at de Green," said Hardy. A little smirk pulled at the corner of his mouth, and he looked at Landon.

"Wid de Auctor's help, we did. But dat was just one fight. De prince of darkness is too big for just one fight. So we have to keep fighting."

Landon looked at Hardy as the sea fell and then rose behind him. The sun was coming up, he could tell, but it was hidden by a gauzelike haze. A definite reddish tint colored the air.

Red sky at morning, sailors take warning.

"We have to keep fighting," said Landon. The words made him feel both tired—as if he had a very long journey ahead of him—and hopeful, hopeful that one day the battle would finally be won.

The ark was well ahead of them and was folding up its "wings"—the batlike sails that extended out from its sides. It continued to drift, however, between two towers of dark rock. It disappeared from view.

"Dere's a beach in dere," said Hardy. "Only place we can load de aminals."

If we find them, Landon thought.

"We have to anchor out here," said Hardy. "And go in on de jolly boat."

Landon looked at the boat strung up behind them. It looked solid and seaworthy enough, yet the thought of leaving the big ship made him feel exposed and vulnerable.

"What about the cannons?" he asked, hoping to change the plan. "Won't we want the thunder guns by the ark? For protection?"

"Too dangerous," said Hardy. "One dunder shot might scare de aminals and scatter dem. We want to get dem out as quietlike as we can."

A strange sound caused Landon to start. He looked back. A sail was going up, rising and collapsing like a shade. And then another and another. Down below, Battleroot and Wagglewhip were working the ropes. They were incredibly quick and strong. When all the sails had been raised, the two men approached an iron lever that looked stuck between cogs of a rusty half wheel rising from the deck. They grabbed the lever together and pulled it out from the wheel. Their grunts and groans were quickly drowned out by a clattering, rumbling noise that reverberated through the planks. They were dropping anchor.

"It's time," said Hardy slowly when the ship had come to a lolling pause, "to draw our swords and go ashore."

Without waiting for Landon to reply, Hardy headed off and disappeared below deck. Holly was up on the bridge, her blond hair tied back in a ponytail. She was staring at the island. Bridget and Melech stood just outside the captain's corridor. They, too, were staring ahead while Epops nonchalantly fluffed his wings and groomed himself. Landon went down and was surprised to find Hardy drawing not one or two swords, but eleven of them. He was happy to give four of them to Landon, which he somehow managed to carry up the ladder.

"Why do we need so many?" Landon asked between breaths. Though he was trying to be careful, the swords clattered noisily when he set them on the deck.

"Two each for me and Wagglewhop. One for everyone else dat's able-handed. And a spare."

Landon still wore his scabbard from last night, though he really had not intended to use it. Was he really going to carry a sword in it now?

"But we're not all going on to the island, are we?"

Hardy held two swords in a big X. In a flash, he twirled them about like propellers and slid them into two scabbards before Landon could even blink.

"Into de island"—Hardy hoisted his pack onto his back and cinched it by bouncing up and down—"is you, me, and Wagglewhop." He looked Landon in the eye. "And Melech."

Landon blinked. "We're leaving my sisters out here?"

"Battleroot stay here. Little misses go to de beach. Wait wid Vates."

Landon sighed. It was hard to decide which seemed more dangerous—the anchored ship or the exposed ark—but he felt better knowing his sisters would be onshore with Vates and Ditty.

Ditty. . .

With no one needed at the helm, they all gathered on the deck near the jolly boat, and Hardy explained the plan. At least as much as he had shared with Landon of the plan. As for the rest of the rescue plan, well, that seemed to remain up to the Auctor. They would be going in by faith. *And praying,* Landon thought as he listened to Hardy's pep talk, *that we'll know what to do once we get there.*

"I don't like it."

Everyone looked at Holly.

The ship gently creaked. Its motion was so mild compared to before that it almost felt as if they were already on land.

"I don't like staying on the beach, I mean," she said, looking around at the group. "I want to be there to count the animals when they get on the ark, of course." She smiled at Landon, and he couldn't help smiling back. "But I don't want to miss out on the action on the island, either." She gave Hardy a tough look, though it didn't seemed to faze him.

Landon cleared his throat. He remembered her joining him to seek out Malus Quidam's shadows in the dark woods. The girl seemed fairly fearless, if not a bit stubborn and foolhardy. He didn't feel it was his call here, however, to invite her or not. Hardy seemed in charge of this operation.

"Can you lift your sword?" Landon asked. It was the first question that came to mind. Though he wasn't trying to consciously test her or dissuade her, it seemed an appropriate question. Then again, maybe it wasn't fair. Landon could hardly manage his own sword without using two hands.

Holly glared at him. Gripping the handle of her sword with one hand, she slowly drew it out. She raised it up. As she held it over her head, her arm straight and only barely trembling, the group collectively gasped. *She did it.* Landon felt a strange mixture of pride and awe. He resisted the temptation to lift his own sword to see if he could hold it so motionlessly. This was incredible.

And then, her eyes growing rapidly wider, Holly started falling backward. It was like watching something in slow motion. A gleam traveled down the steel blade as it drifted. Holly's locked arm followed. And then her terror-stricken face. She fell to the deck like a clanging board.

Landon was the first to kneel beside her. "Are you okay? I'm sorry, Holly. I didn't mean to—"

"Hey," she said, moving only her eyes and mouth. Her body remained as rigid as the Statue of Liberty. "If you have to use this thing out there, then I don't want to go, after all. Okay?"

Landon sighed. "It might be dangerous."

Her head moved in a barely perceptible nod. "You be careful, okay, Landon? I want to count you when you come back, too." Her eyes softened and smiled.

"Okay," Landon said. "Do you need a hand getting up?"

Her body tensed, and then Holly grimaced. "Just give me a minute. I can listen from down here."

Bridget's curls hung all around her face as she bowed her head toward her sister. "Don't leave me behind," Bridget said, her voice high and cracking. "I don't want to be left without you *and* Landon."

Holly closed her eyes, and her body relaxed. She opened her eyes and gazed up at her little sister. "I'll stay with you, Bridget. Don't worry. Okay?"

Bridget nodded and sniffed. A tiny tear splattered on the deck. This seemed to loosen Holly even more. Soon she had released the sword and was bending her arm, then her torso, and finally her legs. Landon picked up her sword as she stood. In some strange way, she seemed to be giving him extra strength by agreeing that he should go without her. Both her sword and the sword hanging from his belt suddenly felt a pound lighter.

"Okay, men." Hardy was waving at Wagglewhip and Battleroot, directing them as they hoisted the jolly boat over the side and then began releasing the ropes through the pulleys. Once it was in the water, they threw down their own hooked ropes, catching the boat and pulling it alongside the ship. Landon swallowed as the realization became more real. *We're actually going to do this. We're going to the island of shadows and Arcans. The Island of Arcanum.*

Next the two stout men lowered a knotted-rope ladder to the boat. Hardy gave everyone a nod and swiftly clambered overboard. It was decided that Landon should go next, staying close to Bridget as she descended after him. Then came Holly, insisting that she felt limber and fine.

Everyone was sitting, as Hardy instructed them to do, and watching, craning their necks as a burlap-wrapped cluster of swords descended. Hardy stood, reaching to pull it in, tucking it under a small shelf at the front of the boat. Then he undid the pulley ropes, and the boat leaned harder against the ship. The rubbing wood groaned and screeched. A couple minutes later, down came Melech, his massive form slowly twisting. Landon stood this time to help Hardy guide the horse to the space at the back.

"Hi, Melech," said Bridget.

"Hello, little miss."

The pulley ropes went up. After Wagglewhip climbed down as carefully and easily as a spider, the hooked ropes were released, and the boat, which was now a very full vessel, began to drift apart from the ship. Landon looked at the ladder hanging along the ship's side. This was his first view of the ship from the outside, he realized. It was quite an impressive—and beautiful—sight. To either side of the rope ladder were evenly spaced squares—the cannon positions. The masts rose high into the air above the body of the ship like straight, bare tree limbs draped with sails and strung with ropes. The once reddish sky had turned more pink and gray. Landon felt a slight shiver, although he didn't feel cold. A lump formed in Landon's throat as he watched the big ship recede behind them. Soon Battleroot's waving arm was no longer visible. As Landon turned forward to see twin cliffs rise on either side, another lump formed. This one in the pit of his stomach. Everyone in the boat remained quiet, listening only to the dip of the oars and the splashes along the sides as Hardy and Wagglewhip rowed the boat toward the beach.

Chapter Thirteen

The reunion on the beach was brief, but it was heavenly. Landon hugged Vates for a long time.

"I thought you were Noah at first," Landon said with a little laugh.

"Noah? Do I really look that old?" Vates' white hair and weather-creased skin seemed to fit with the ruggedness of their surroundings. His eyes sparkled as joyfully and deeply as ever. He held Landon by the shoulders. "It is good to see you again, Landon."

Landon almost had to choke back his emotion. "You, too," he said weakly. Something about Vates' presence could make Landon feel happy and sad, strong and weak, all at the same time. Landon introduced Vates to Bridget, and then he turned his attention to the other friend he'd been waiting to see again.

Ditty.

"Hi," Landon said, standing straight and tall. He angled out his hip that carried the sword.

"Hi, Landon," said Ditty. Her hair seemed a bit longer than he'd remembered, and she appeared a little taller, too. He'd grown in the meantime even more than she had, however.

Landon held out his hand. As soon as she touched it, he felt his energy drain from his body. He realized, too, that the firm, unmoving land beneath him felt stranger than the ship. His body wanted to lean back and forth, and so he felt unsteady. Before he realized what he was saying, the words slipped out. "I feel dizzy," he said squeezing her hand.

Ditty giggled, the sound lighter than the foam washing up onshore. "The sea will do that to you. We've been on land a little longer than you have. And the ark doesn't rock too much. There's something called a stabilizer attached underwater to the keel." Seeing uncertainty in Landon's eyes, she added, "Vates told me about it."

"He sure knows a lot of stuff," said Landon, thinking his own speech was sounding painfully dull.

"He's amazing," said Ditty, flaring her eyes on *maze*. "And you know what?"

They were still holding hands. The energy that had seemed to drain from his body now seemed to be flowing back in—through Ditty's touch.

"What?" said Landon, feeling stronger and steadier.

"He thinks that you might know how to break the spell."

Landon's bewilderment returned. He relaxed his grip on her hand.

"What? What spell?" He could feel his skin tighten between his eyebrows.

"The spell of Chief Arcanum on the animals." Ditty whispered this as if Arcans might be lurking in the shadows.

The shadows. . .

Landon glanced inland, but the cliffs were too high all around them to see the funneling "smoke" he'd seen from the ship.

"I hadn't heard anything about a spell."

Ditty nodded. "I know. We've all been learning a lot of new things fast. Even Ludo is having a hard time remembering. Well"—Ditty's face twitched and she looked at the sand—"it's hard for him in a painful way. He feels so responsible. And guilty for sending the animals. . .here."

Ludo. . .

Landon looked around. There were Vates, Hardy, Melech, Wagglewhip, Holly, and Bridget—and Epops, who had chosen to fly rather than ride in the boat to the island. A long ramp about ten feet wide ran up from the beach to the gaping doorway of the ark. In the dark opening stood a solitary figure. Landon remembered how happy Ludo had been once the spell of the gold coin—and the lure of the shadows—had been removed from him. Apparently, that feeling hadn't lasted too long once the realization had set in of what he had done.

Landon felt sad, too, looking up at him. He didn't know whether he should wave or go up to Ludo, but then the figure disappeared into the ark.

Landon sighed. "We have to get those animals, don't we?" He was speaking to himself more than Ditty. "Otherwise things will never be the same again—in Wonderwood. It'll be almost as bad as the shadows."

"The Auctor does have a plan. You believe that, don't you?"

Landon looked at Ditty. Then he glanced back at the ark. The vessel was huge. Its wooden body dominated the beach, filling the space within this rocky cove. But in a sense, it only seemed to fill it with more emptiness. He thought about Noah building an ark like this on dry land. Why? Because God had told him to build it. Because it was part of God's plan.

"I hope so," said Landon. He looked at Ditty. "Yes, I think so. I believe the Auctor has a plan for us to get the animals." He just wished he knew a little more about what the plan was.

"I've already been asking him for help. And I'll keep asking."

"Thanks," said Landon.

The next instant, Ditty was hugging him, and Landon thought he'd be able to fly right there from the beach to the top of the cliff. He wouldn't mind feeling this way forever. But then she let go, and he breathed again.

"Thanks," he said.

The group formed a circle on the beach and knelt in the sand holding hands. Vates said a few words aloud, but mostly they stayed quiet, listening to the surf and the hollow echo off the surrounding rocks. Beyond those sounds, they also listened for something else. For someone else. And deep in his soul, Landon felt that he could hear him.

I wouldn't mind feeling this way forever, either, Landon thought.

Unfortunately, they had to break the circle and get under way. Hardy strode back to the jolly boat, stooped over it, and returned carrying two lanterns.

"Where'd you get those?" said Landon. "I mean, how'd they get in the boat?"

"Packed dem in last night," said Hardy. "You were sleeping."

Landon nodded. "Good thinking." Although, since it was daytime, he didn't understand why they would need lanterns.

As if on cue, the group separated into two parties. Hardy, Wagglewhip, Melech, and Landon started walking up the beach. The others gathered between the ramp and the jolly boat, watching them go. Landon tried not to look back too much. He wondered how on earth they were going to get up and over this steep cliff. They passed a large opening in the rock wall that appeared strangely bright inside. Landon paused, wondering, but then hurried to catch up with the others. Beyond an outcropping that looked like a big black foot, they came to another hole. This one, however, seemed dark and dank.

Wagglewhip started in.

They weren't going to climb the cliff after all. They were going through it.

"Hey," said Landon, flinching at the ring of his voice down the tunnel.

Wagglewhip turned as the others looked back.

"What about that other cave?" said Landon hopefully. "That one looked. . .nicer."

Wagglewhip shook his head. "Dead end, that one. Doesn't go through. Need this one to reach the animals."

Landon sighed and nodded. Then he glanced back over the jagged toe of the giant rock foot. Feeling heavier than he could remember, Landon raised his hand in a wave of farewell. Holly stood with her arm around Bridget, and both waved. Ditty stood between Bridget and Vates, waving. Vates raised his staff and gave one slow nod.

Beyond the gathering on the beach, something else caught Landon's eye. He squinted toward the top of the ramp, where Ludo had reappeared. Ludo raised one hand, held it, and then lowered it again.

Landon lifted his own hand another notch before heading into the tunnel.

As he entered, darkness engulfed him. Ahead of him, two flames burst to life, and a new world appeared. Pointed rocks rose from the ground and hung from the ceiling, dripping. It was like walking through the salivating jaws of a monster. *Stalactites and stalagmites,* Landon thought. It helped to keep his mind occupied. *Which one is which? I always forget.* Some of the mineral formations had connected to form slim, tapered columns. The lantern lights swung and bounced ahead of him. Landon couldn't imagine going in here without them. *Good thinking, indeed, Hardy!*

Something started nagging at Landon. As he pondered it, he wondered why it hadn't nagged at him earlier. If this was where they had taken all of the animals from Wonderwood—where were they?

Where are the animals?

The thought that followed this one, of course, was *where are the Arcans?*

And then the final thought, a thought that Landon was glad hadn't occurred to him on the beach with Ditty: *Could Ditty's parents really be here? Are they alive? Do we really want to find them—dead* or *alive?*

Landon tried not to worry too much over any of these questions. For now, it was enough to concentrate on staying together in the cave and making it through to wherever it was they were going.

The air was cool, musty, and damp—much different from the thick, salty air of the sea. After traveling through a long stretch of tunnel ranging from perhaps fifteen to twenty feet high, the ceiling rose to a cavernous height too far up to be reached by lantern light. The walls spread far away. It was like walking in a huge, empty arena. The air remained cool but became less damp. It felt, and smelled, fresh. Although not necessarily forest fresh. More like open-air rock fresh. But then, with the very next breath, it seemed the air changed entirely.

Landon began to choke and gasp. He heard the others coughing, as well. The air that seemed fresh was but a tiny trickle, overwhelmed by such a pungent, powerful mix of smells and odors that it almost made Landon retch. He lifted his arm to his nose, trying to shield or filter some of the smell. He was squinting, too, as if confronted by stinging smoke or burning fumes. What if the fumes were poisonous?

No, something told him. Though the stench was powerful, it wouldn't hurt him.

But it's so bad!

The party had stopped, and Wagglewhip turned to face them. His eyes glistened in the lantern light. "Getting close," he said, his own voice muffled by his sleeve. "Be on the lookout."

Lookout for what? Landon wondered, but he said nothing aloud. It was difficult enough just to breathe. He tried to close off his nose and use only his mouth. The air even tasted nasty.

A mild explosion sounded as Melech let out a sneeze. He was wagging his head back and forth as if to clear away the smell. The poor horse couldn't cover his nose with an arm or sleeve. And his nostrils were so big!

"Putrid!" Melech announced in disgust. "Foul smell!"

"Shh!" Hardy pushed one finger to his mouth then petted Melech's mane. "Dere, dere horsey. Must not shout. Must not—wah-*choo*!" Hardy covered his mouth with his arm, his eyes bulging.

Landon tried thinking of flowers or his mother's perfume, but it didn't work. "What is it?" he said. "That smell?"

Wagglewhip gave him a steady gaze. In a sad, quiet voice he said, "It's the animals. And the smell of burning flesh, if you could call it flesh."

Landon held his breath a moment. He didn't have any pets. But he'd been to a friend's house that had a guinea pig and a dog. One time, the guinea pig's cage hadn't been cleaned out in some time, and it stunk. Another time, Landon stepped in dog poop in the backyard. He remembered feeling a little nauseous as he scraped it from his shoe. Now imagine the stink a whole forest's worth of animals could produce if they were trapped and their cages were never cleaned out.

And burning flesh? Landon was almost afraid to ask. It turned out he didn't have to—Hardy asked first.

"Are dey cooking our aminals?" He clenched his fist over his mouth.

Melech stopped wagging his head. "Why would they—would they do such a thing?"

Wagglewhip sighed. "They might." He glanced at Hardy and then at Melech, clearing his throat. "We used to cook some animals, too. Only certain kinds. For, uh, food."

Melech took a step back, retreating from the lantern light.

Landon stepped toward his friend, forgetting about the smell. He rubbed Melech's nose and then up between his ears. He'd never seen Melech's ears so flat.

"In my world, we eat some animals, too. But none like you. You will never be eaten, Melech. I promise you."

Melech snorted and half turned his head. After a moment, he looked back at Landon. "Well, I should certainly hope not. After all we have been through together. . ."

Landon smiled and hugged the horse's neck.

Wagglewhip cleared his throat somewhat uncomfortably again. "The smell of animals cooking is, uh, *good.* It smells good."

Melech jerked his head back, looking at Landon.

Landon pressed his lips together and smiled grimly. Then he nodded. "He's right. There's nothing better than bacon sizzling or steak being grilled or—well, he's right." Landon turned to Wagglewhip. "But this is a bad smell. So if it's not from animals—"

Landon gasped and then choked and gagged. The full force of the stench hit him like a giant hand knocking him sideways.

If they're not burning animals. . .

Tears welled up in his eyes, blurring his vision and stinging. "No!" Landon said. "They can't be!"

The others stared at him.

"Can't be what?" Hardy took a step toward him, swinging the lantern.

Landon could hardly get the words out. He wanted to turn back and run. Run to the salty sea air and get back on the ship and never see these Arcans—they were monsters!

"Ditty's. . ." A chest convulsion hitched his voice. He gulped for air, horrid as it was. "Her parents!"

Wagglewhip's eyes flared wide but then relaxed. He actually seemed to be sighing with relief. Was he a monster, too?

"No," said Wagglewhip shaking his head. "Don't think it's them we smell." He snorted, clearing his nose. Then he rolled back his sleeve and held the lantern over his arm. In the strange light, Landon didn't see anything. Then his memory came up with it, and there it was. A crude tattoo of a skull over two crossed bones.

Landon frowned. "That was *burned* on your arm? But. . . who would they be tattooing today?"

When Wagglewhip responded, a chill ran up Landon's spine. "Each other."

Gradually, the great space began to shrink. Soon their lanterns were illuminating a rock wall on either side and a jagged ceiling overhead. Landon noticed, however, that there weren't any more stalactites or stalagmites. They were moving through a different kind of tunnel. He wondered if this one had been fashioned by human—or Arcan—hands.

Why would they burn one another's flesh? What kind of creatures are they?

Landon trembled.

With a quick intake of air, he ground to a halt.

There was something about the walls—

The walls were moving!

The others seemed to have noticed, as well. The party slowed and then paused, looking about.

The walls were breaking apart and shifting in a thousand pieces. A clattering noise filled the tunnel. At first, Landon wondered if his eyes might be playing tricks on him. Then he thought maybe they were just shadows. Except they weren't moving in relation to the gently swinging lanterns. They were moving on their own.

Oh no. The shadows of Malus Quidam.

But what about that strange noise? Something seemed different. Movement from the floor caught Landon's eye, and he looked down. His body went rigid with fear, all except his thumping heart. A stone was moving near his foot!

Landon watched in frozen horror and then slowly breathed as the stone skittered *away* from him. *Thank goodness!*

The stone had legs. Two tiny claws came out.

Though Landon had never seen one of these creatures before, he suddenly knew what he was looking at. His fear turned to excitement. He almost wanted to laugh for joy.

"They're crabs!" he said, his voice hissing among the rattle of tiny legs. "We've found our first animals!"

"Ugh," said Hardy raising his lantern and grimacing. "Dese not from Wonderwood. We didn't come here for dese."

"Oh," said Landon. Despite Hardy's disappointment, it was nice seeing something else that was alive.

The crabs continued to scatter as the party moved on. Either the bad smell was getting better, or Landon was becoming so accustomed to it that it only seemed to be getting better. Either way, he was glad not to be choking and gagging on it anymore.

Without warning, Wagglewhip stopped. "Douse your lamp!" He said this and then followed his own command. Hardy blew at his light, and the world went dark. The clattering of crabs slowed to a trickle of ticks. Landon groped at the air around him. When his hand found a familiar flank—*Melech*—he sighed with relief. It felt good to be connected to someone in the dark.

"What is it?" he whispered, wondering if anyone else could hear his heart beating.

"Shush," said Wagglewhip. "Something's coming."

Some*thing*? That didn't sound good.

The seconds passed like minutes. The sound of his own breathing seemed loud to Landon. And he wished he could muffle the thumping in his chest.

Melech's body tensed. It was painful—listening, sniffing, watching the darkness—waiting. Unconsciously, Landon's free hand moved to the hilt of his sword.

A faint glow appeared ahead. Then he saw a dot of light behind the glow.

Landon was aware of his sword now. His fingers curled around the handle. Something told him not to unsheathe it, however. *Not yet. . .*

"To de side," said Hardy. "Get to de side."

Landon half pushed, half followed Melech toward the wall. As he pressed his shoulder to the rocks, he hoped a crab wouldn't retaliate by pinching him.

The light was drawing nearer like a silent, slow-moving train. When Landon found his voice, he asked, "Should we run?"

A second later, Wagglewhip replied, "No. We wait. This is the only way in from the beach. We have to face them sooner or later." He sighed.

Landon swallowed. He softly patted Melech's hide, though he was really trying to comfort himself. He thought of his sisters and Vates and Ditty on the beach. *They're asking the Auctor to help us.* A strange calm seeped into his heart as he watched the light. He thought of the firefly lantern Ditty had showed him when they first met. And he smiled. Pretty soon they would be able to see whatever was carrying the light. Shortly after that, of course, whatever was carrying the light would also be able to see them.

There appeared to be two figures behind the light. Landon counted four skinny legs. As he held his breath for the faces to emerge, the light stopped.

"Are you sure, Buttercake, are you sure?"

Buttercake? The voice sounded like a woman's.

"Yes! Yes! It's a ship, I'm telling you. A *ship!* And not an Arcan rig. Gingerpie, I would not tease about this."

Gingerpie? A male voice said this.

"What if it's not there? What if it's not at the beach?"

Silence.

"I saw it from the high cliff on the far side of the island last night. I think it was circling us. There's only one place for it to land."

"But what if it's not there?"

A pause. "We have to find out, don't we? We have to go look."

"But if it's *not* there. . .and they find out we've left the keep and the tunnels—" The woman's voice broke off.

"I know. But we have to hope and trust. We have to believe."

A loud sniff. "Okay."

"Okay?"

"Okay."

The light advanced—a flickering flame—and the figures came more fully into view. The man wasn't much taller than

Hardy or Wagglewhip, but he was much skinnier. His skin clung to his bones like wet clothing. His hair was a thick, long, matted nest, as was his beard. His clothes—well, they were hardly clothes at all. He was wearing rags, bits of cloth and other material stitched together. The man holding the small torch was easier to see. The sight of him made Landon feel a little sick to his stomach.

The woman came into view.

She wore no beard, of course, though her hair was as thick and long and as nasty as the man's. She was nearly as skinny, too, although her facial features appeared a bit softer and fuller and therefore were less unsettling.

They were so close now. Crabs were scattering. For a moment, Landon almost thought—and for some reason feared—that the pair of strange, skinny creatures might actually walk right by without noticing them. The glow of their light washed over Wagglewhip and Hardy, who were both crouched and still as boulders. Then the light hit Melech and Landon. That's when it stopped.

Landon blinked, breathless. He released his sword, raising his hand to shield his eyes from the flame's bright glow. The man and the woman were staring at Melech as if Landon wasn't even there. But Landon was staring at the woman's face. Her eyes. . .

"It's not in the keep with the others," said the man.

"It's so—so *big*. So healthy."

"It's not afraid."

"It doesn't know. It's new here. . ."

Landon felt like a ghost. It was as if they really couldn't see him.

The man and the woman looked at each other. The man's sunken eyes grew wide. "They can't be, can they?"

"Sending more here?" asked the woman. "But who? And from where? There's not any room." Her head bowed, slowly shaking. "We can't do this, Buttercake. *I* can't. . .not anymore." She stepped into him, trembling.

"Excuse me," said Landon. He almost wanted to hug them, but he was afraid they might break in his grasp.

The woman looked up at the man as if he had spoken. He merely held her.

"Excuse me," said Landon. "Over here."

Hardy and Wagglewhip were standing now, still quiet and unseen.

The man and the woman both slowly turned their heads. Their gaze grazed Landon but settled on Melech.

"Can't you see me?" Landon brought up his hand and wiggled his fingers. "Right here." He reached toward them, but they didn't react until his hand passed by the torch.

The man jumped back and dropped the torch. It crashed, and blackness engulfed them.

"I'm sorry!" said Landon. "I'm not trying to hurt you—"

"It's not a shadow!" The man's voice whispered. It sounded as if he and the woman were scurrying away, scraping at the walls like two giant crabs seeking to escape.

Not a shadow? What on earth?

"No, I'm not a shadow," said Landon. "Hardy, can you light—"

A quick scratch sounded, and then a flame sputtered to life. Hardy touched the flame to the lantern wick.

The man and the woman were backed against the opposite wall, their knees and elbows sticking out. The woman's eyes were even larger now. They flicked back and forth between Wagglewhip, Hardy, and Landon, ignoring Melech.

"What do you want?" she said. "What are you? Why have you come to this place of death?"

Landon eased forward and squatted. He kept his hands on his legs. "I'm not a shadow," he repeated. He didn't understand what was happening, but somehow this seemed important to get across. "I'm not a shadow."

The woman's gaze met his and stopped. Her eyes appeared to be pulsing—with fear, with repulsion, and finally, with a gradual glimmer of comprehension.

"You're not a shadow," she said evenly. "You. . .are. . .not. . . a. . .shadow."

Landon stared back, his eyes throbbing with a different sort of recognition.

"You're Ditty's mother." He drew a deep breath. "You. . . are. . .Ditty's. . . mother."

Chapter Fifteen

There was much to talk about and to catch up on. Too much, in fact, to cover while standing in the middle of a tunnel crawling with crabs. When Ditty's mother and father—for that's who they were—learned that their daughter was waiting on the beach, they took off running toward the cavern, plunging into the darkness.

"Wait!" Wagglewhip called after them. "We need to get the animals. And we could use your help."

The couple dragged themselves back, looking very sad. "That may be impossible," said the man. "They're trapped. Imprisoned."

"We can snap de bars wid dese," said Hardy, brandishing one of his swords.

"There are no bars," explained the man, "only shadows."

Wagglewhip and Hardy looked at each other. "So"—Wagglewhip eyed the man warily—"all the easier then. Just show us where they are."

"No," said the woman. She glanced from Wagglewhip to

Landon, her eyes pleading. "Shadows are worse than bars. The animals obey the shadows. There's no escaping them."

"You see," the man broke in, "Chief Arcanum cast a curse. Once, the animals were immune to the shadows, but here they can only succumb to them."

Landon thought of something. "Ditty set me free from the spell of the gold coin," he said. "Maybe we should go get her and bring her here. Maybe she'll know what to do!"

Ditty's mother and father looked at him with eagerness and astonishment. "She did that?" said her father. "Our little Ditty?"

Landon nodded. "She's not that little now."

Her parents smiled. The sight of their teeth made Landon remember how skinny they looked. And how hungry they must be.

"No," said Hardy.

Everyone looked at him.

"Vates said you would break de curse here, Landon. Ditty to stay on de beach. Dis is your mission."

Landon frowned. "I want to help, but I don't know what to do."

"It will come," Hardy said. "You had de vision."

"Yeah," Landon said. "The vision." He was feeling uncomfortable. His crazy vision didn't seem to have anything to do with any of this, other than the coincidence that he had seen animals and those were what they had come here to rescue. The grins on the faces of Ditty's parents vanished, but the couple still looked hungry.

"What do you eat here?" asked Landon. He wanted to

change the subject, but he was also quite curious. "How have you survived?" He hoped they weren't eating the Wonderwood animals. Then again, if that was the only way they could survive. . .

With alarming speed, the man stepped to the wall, snatched a crab from it, and threw it to the ground. The crab's shell cracked, and a claw fell off. The creature was dead. Before Landon could speak, the man had scooped up a chunk of shell and tipped it to his mouth, slurping. The man gave another piece to his wife, and she sipped from it, as well.

Landon's stomach turned.

"Would you like some?" the man offered.

"Um, no thanks." Landon decided he would be more careful with his questions from now on. Maybe there were some things he'd rather not know about.

"The Auctor provides," said the woman, chewing.

"The Auctor provides," said the man solemnly. "Although it's been hard eating only crab goo all this time. Runs right through you; doesn't stick to the ribs much." He grinned and gestured to his skeletal form. Creamy liquid dribbled down his chin.

Landon had to look away.

He and his sisters knew about living on oranges, bread, and ginger ale for two days. He couldn't imagine eating only one food for years. Especially crab goo. He may have just permanently lost his appetite for seafood.

"It's not only food that the Auctor provides," Ditty's mother said after she'd swallowed. It appeared hard for her to get it down, despite how hungry she must be. "He also gives us hope."

Ditty's father nodded. "That's how we've really survived here. *Hope*. You are the answer to our hope."

Landon didn't feel like anyone's answer to hope. He only felt a little scared and uncertain. He could use some hope himself.

"We're not out yet," said Wagglewhip grimly. "First we have to go in. Show us the way."

They strode down the tunnel in the direction Ditty's parents had come from. Landon couldn't imagine their pain right now, knowing their long-lost daughter was so close yet still so far. He hoped they would all get to see her again when this was over. He decided to try to keep things light in the meantime.

"So," he said as they walked along, "your names are Buttercake and Gingerpie?"

The man and woman looked at each other, slowing a few steps, and frowned. Then they burst into quiet laughter.

Landon felt his face grow warm. What was so funny? Now he felt awkward and uncomfortable, but the sound of their soft giggling began to loosen his heart, nonetheless. Twenty paces later, they were still shaking with laughter, touching each other and setting off more twitters.

Goodness, Landon thought, *it's like they haven't had a good laugh in. . .years.* He sighed with pity. What misery they must have been living through! Being trapped on a dreadful island with no other valley folk for company. Not seeing their daughter grow up. Dwelling in these damp tunnels and eating that runny crab glop. . .

And Landon knew that probably wasn't the worst of it. The worst was probably the flesh-burning Arcans. What would they be like? Curiosity and dread filled Landon at the thought of the mysterious beings. It seemed his curiosity would soon be satisfied.

Ditty's mother and father finally quit laughing, though their eyes still glistened with tears. Their torch had been rekindled from Hardy's lantern, and they lowered the burning stick. The party slowed. Ahead, the tunnel banked to the right. Before they reached the curve, Ditty's father smashed the torch against the floor, snuffing the flame. The others turned, forming a half circle around them. In the remaining lantern light, the skinny man said, "We're almost there." He sniffed at the air, animal-like. "The burning's done. Now the dancing will begin."

Dancing?

The man's eyes peered at Landon from their hollows. "Sorry for laughing. Your question took us by surprise. I call my wife Gingerpie, and she calls me Buttercake." His lips split into a grin, but he didn't laugh. "But our names our Griggory and Dorothy, Griggory and Dorothy Willowbranch." His eyes closed, and a leftover laughter tear squeezed out. He opened his eyes, looking past Landon to some memory. "In the old days, people called us Griggs and Dot of Willowbranch Way."

"I'm Hardy," said Hardy, plunging in his hand. "Hardy Hedgewood of de, uh, hedgewood."

"Wagglewhip Mossyrock. Used to live downriver. I miss the beavers." He sniffed.

"And this is Melech," said Landon, happy to introduce his friend to Ditty's parents. "Melech. . .Knightleap from the chess-board in the sky."

Landon smiled at their bewildered expressions. "It's a long story." He patted Melech's neck.

"And you are?" asked Griggs.

"Oh!" Landon's face warmed. "I'm Landon Snow of. . . Button Up—whoops! I mean Minneapolis, Minnesota."

They nodded politely. "Sounds nice."

Landon's face throbbed with heat. "It is."

"Well it is very nice to meet you all," said Dot. "I do wish we could offer you some tea and berry—" Her voice broke off, and she turned away.

Landon felt a catch in his throat and concentrated on holding back the tears.

"You will, lady, you will," said Hardy. "Back in Willowbranch Way. Now, let's get de aminals and get out of here." It was the first time Landon had ever heard Hardy's voice crack with emotion.

Are we really going to make it back? Landon closed his eyes. *Please be with us, and help us!*

"What have they done to them?"

At the sound of Melech's steady voice, everyone flinched. Dot and Griggs actually jumped backward, and Griggs fell down.

"It—the horse—it talks!"

Landon looked at them in surprise as they scrambled back up, stepping cautiously closer. Landon felt the need to explain. "He's a very special horse from a magical place outside of Wonderwood. Can't the other animals talk?" It seemed a silly question. He hadn't actually expected any other animals to talk. The words just came out.

"Not like that. Not like *we* do," said Griggs as he and Dot drew closer still. Together, they reached out bony hands to touch the amazing Melech. As they gently stroked the sides of his head,

Melech whinnied agreeably. "Our animals, the animals here, well, they do understand things. They can communicate in their own way. But. . ."

Landon waited. "But what?"

Griggs paused, holding his hand still near Melech's neck. "But they've been put under a curse to hear only one voice."

A musty draft blew through, carrying the stench of hundreds of soiled animals. And worse. . .

"They can hear only one voice?"

Softly, Dot whispered, "Chief Arcanum's."

A strange feeling clawed its way up Landon's back. *A curse. . . one voice. . .Chief Arcanum.* It made no sense to him, yet something seemed to be dawning in the back of his mind.

Griggs released his hand from Melech. After glancing at Landon and the others, Griggs slowly lowered his head. "It's no use trying to get the animals. They'll never come. They're ensnared by the shadows and captivated—truly held in captivity—by the chief's voice. He's the only one they'll ever obey."

"Can you explain 'chief'?" asked Melech. "What is this person?"

"He's the leader," said Griggs, "sort of like a king, or—"

Melech pranced stiffly in place, snorting. "Like a king, you say. I fled a wayward king once before. Perhaps now it is time to face one."

Griggs stared a moment and then bowed and shook his head. Dot stroked Melech soothingly. Sadness seemed to weigh heavily on Ditty's parents.

"It is no use, I'm afraid." Griggs sighed. "We—Dot and I—we thought we could help the animals. We thought we could take care of them, and then someday"—he glanced up—"our hope and help would come rescue us all. But," he said, looking back down, "we learned that it's impossible. If we go in there, we will risk all of our lives for nothing. We thought—" his voice dropped. Finally, he looked up with more sadness and pain in his eyes than Landon had ever seen. "We thought you were coming to rescue *us*."

Dot stopped petting Melech and looked at her husband. "Only us," she said.

"Why is it impossible?" said Landon. "Isn't there a way to break the curse?"

Griggs looked at him. "Yes and no. The only way to break it is to know the words and speak them to the animals yourself. That will reverse it. But there is a problem."

Landon leaned closer. His fingers curled around the hilt of his sword. "What's that?"

"To know the words, you must listen to the chief speak them. He repeats them every night after the dance. And if you listen to the chief speak them, you fall under the curse yourself."

Well, that did seem to present a problem. The cogs in Landon's mind began to grind. There had to be a way to solve this. *I have to figure this one out. Vates and Hardy—they're all counting on me. I had a vision. . .*

Landon realized something. Studying the sickly pair in the flickering torch light with a wary eye, he asked, "How come you aren't under the curse? You just said he repeats it every night after the dance. But you have never heard it for yourself?" Landon's fingers tightened their grip on his sword.

The two figures appeared even sadder. Griggs finally looked

at Landon, his eyes glistening once again. "Another did hear it." He sighed. "He was from the Cottonwood clan. He told us he had heard the chief's curse and was about to tell us the words when he. . .when his throat tightened up, and he fell over, gasping and coughing. Before he died, he put his fingers in his ears and croaked two words: *'Don't listen.'*"

Landon let go of his sword and let his shoulders sag. "I'm sorry."

"De Cottonwoods," Hardy muttered. "Dey're a good bunch."

One question still lingered in Landon's mind. "So how have you never heard it, after all this time?"

Heaving a sigh, Griggs stepped to the wall and proceeded to peel something from it. It wasn't a crab (thank goodness!). He came back holding a layer of spongy green stuff.

Griggs handed his torch to Dot. "Moss," he said, as he tore the square in two and then rolled up each piece. "Form-fitting." He stuffed one piece into his left ear and the other piece into his right. Raising his eyebrows and shrugging his shoulders, he rolled his eyes around and shook his head. In a loud voice, he announced, "Can't hear you—totally deaf!" After removing the earplugs, Griggs smiled wanly at Landon. "The Auctor provides," he said quietly.

The Auctor provides. . .in strange ways.

Griggs tossed aside the tufts of moss. "Only good for one use," he explained. "Have to pick it fresh each time. So"—he eyed each of the visitors in turn—"be ready."

Landon watched as two crabs picked at the disposed earplugs.

Very strange ways indeed.

"What if I heard the curse?" said Melech. "Apparently the other animals have not died. I presume they are not all stuffing their ears." Melech glanced toward the bare strip along the wall. "I am afraid my ears would require a substantial amount of material."

"They're not dead, dead," said Griggs puzzlingly, "although their fate is a living death. That's the evil effect of the curse."

"Well," Melech continued, "I could hear it, and then, since I can talk, I could say it, as well. The animals might follow me."

Hardy and Wagglewhip were staring at Melech, thoughtfully nodding. "He may have a point," said Wagglewhip. "The horse might know what he's talking about."

"I don't know," said Griggs. "I just don't know. I suppose the effect could be different. . . ."

Something wasn't sitting right with Landon, however. He shook his head. "No. I don't think that's how it's supposed to happen. I don't know exactly why, but I just don't think. . .no."

"What is wrong, young Landon?" asked Melech. "I will be glad to do my duty and to try—"

"I know. I know you would, Melech." Landon looked at the horse and smiled. Then a lump thickened in his throat, dragging down his smile. "I don't want you to die."

"I would prefer life over death, as well," said Melech. "Though it hardly seems right for one horse to live while so many other animals—"

"I know," said Landon. "I mean, I don't really know. It's just. . ." He sighed in exasperation.

"What is it?" asked Hardy, encouraging him. "What are you dinking about dis?"

Landon gazed at Hardy, knowing he might understand. "I had a vision," said Landon, "of animals. And"—he took a deep breath—"and of something else. I think. I'm trying to remember." He closed his eyes to concentrate.

"Someding else. . . ," Hardy said slowly, as if this might help.

Landon shook his head. It was no use. He opened his eyes. "We just have to go," he said. "We have to go to the animals. . . on faith." Everything in him was screaming not to do this, to get away while they could and not put everyone at risk. Everything, that is, except for one soft little voice. The voice reminded him of Vates—and even Hardy and Melech and Ditty—yet it was much deeper and quieter.

Trust me.

"So how do we get there?" asked Landon, feigning great resolve. "Take us to the animals."

Griggs and Dot hesitated a moment, looking at him. "Our little Ditty saved you from a spell?" It was Dot, a steadiness to her gaze.

"Yes," said Landon. "With a *snap snap* and a *clap clap* and a *tap tap*." He smiled. "She saved me from a spell."

"And now you're going to save all of us," said Dot. It sounded like both a statement and a question.

Landon sighed. "With a lot of help from above."

"And from us," said Wagglewhip stepping forward and raising his lantern.

Landon looked at him. "Exactly."

"When I came in here before," said Wagglewhip, "I got

only as far as the fire pit. That's where I left the animals. I didn't see where they took them from there." He hung his head in shame.

"It's just on the other side," said Griggs, "around the fire pit to the animal keep. Follow me. I'll show you the way."

Chapter Sixteen

They followed the cavelike tunnel to the right, slowing as they approached a very dark opening. As they neared the opening, Landon felt waves of warm air rush past. The darkness itself began to waver and flicker orange, red, and yellow. They stopped at the edge of the opening, and Griggs peeked out. He appeared to be looking downward. He stepped back in and whispered, "Something's different," over his shoulder as he kept his gaze cast outside.

"What is it?" asked Dot.

"I'm not sure," said Griggs. Finally, he turned to face them, and Landon could see fright and concern in his eyes. "They're not dancing. They're doing. . .something else. Everyone stay close to the wall and follow me. We're going around the rim."

Wagglewhip audibly gulped.

Griggs slipped silently around the corner, out into the fluttering darkness. Dot went next, followed by Wagglewhip. Melech glanced back at Landon, and Landon gave him a nod.

No words needed to be spoken. The two friends understood each other. *We're doing our duty,* thought Landon, though he wasn't yet sure if he was glad for it. Melech stepped out and turned left, moving as catlike as a horse could move. A touch on Landon's shoulder had him swivel his head.

"I have your back, young Landon wid de vision."

Hardy stood in a wide stance, his fingers tapping the hilts of his swords like a sheriff handling his holsters.

Landon smiled at him. Despite the pound of trepidation in his stomach, he managed a halfhearted "Thanks." He couldn't help wondering, however, what good his so-called vision would do them. He hadn't wished for any responsibility here. The vision seemed useless and meaningless. *But it means the Auctor has a plan,* he reminded himself. This made him feel a little better, but not much. With a deep breath, Landon stepped around the craggy edge and turned left.

The pathway was plenty wide even for Melech, a span of five or six feet. But the scene that came into view down below was enough to make Landon's head spin. He froze unwillingly and gaped. The darkness that had been wavering and flickering was a gigantic swirl of shadows. *Malus Quidam's shadows.* The twirling funnel rose to an indefinite height overhead, and it tapered somewhat into the pit Landon saw down below. He was standing on a rock ledge that ran around the interior of the crater, perhaps a third of the way up. It was difficult to tell. At the bottom of the black tornado of shadows was a fire. Red, orange, yellow, it glowed. Every now and then, a blue flame shocked the blaze like a lightning bolt. Within these blue flashes, Landon saw them. Tall, humanlike figures gathered round the fire—although they didn't seem human. Even from this distance, the figures' eyes appeared large and black. Each one had something on its head. It was whitish and—Landon gulped—shaped like an animal skull.

A hand gripping his shoulder made Landon gasp. He bit his tongue to keep from yelping. Turning, Landon panted with relief. "Hardy, oh my goodness, you scared me."

"We'd better keep moving," Hardy said softly. "It's safer not to stare."

"Right," Landon said, trying to peel his gaze from the sight below. The figures weren't dancing, but they were doing something around the flames. Then Landon noticed the fire wasn't on the ground but was on a raised circle of stone. The figures stared into the fire, and with each blue flash, they lifted their arms and then brought them down again toward the fire. Their arms and hands were moving about the flames almost as if they were warming themselves. Then it seemed they were actually touching the fire and affecting it. They were shaping it somehow, like a gaseous sculpture.

"Come on," Hardy urged. "Dis is worse dan watching de Coin. Griggs!"

"What?" said Landon, turning.

Griggs had come back for them. "The others have reached the other side," he said. "What are you two doing?"

"I'm scared," said Landon. He gestured with his head. "It looks they're making something."

Griggs glanced over the edge. A blue flash illuminated his face, and his eyes grew wide in the strange light. His expression changed when he looked at Landon. "They're not creatures like you or me, or even the animals. They're agents of Malus Quidam. They're Arcans. Come on." He touched Landon with a bony hand.

As they moved farther along the ledge, Landon heard—and felt—things crunching beneath his boots. He flinched each time at the noise, hoping the Arcans wouldn't hear the sounds down below. At first, Landon assumed he was stepping on rocks, but rocks didn't *crunch* like that. Then he thought they must be crab shells. Except these crunches weren't quite so brittle sounding as the shells. Finally, he paused and stooped for a closer look. As soon as he saw what they were, he wished he hadn't stopped to investigate.

They were bones. Animal bones.

Landon pinched his nose and stood. It was taking all the strength and courage he could muster to keep moving forward. The thought of the beach and the ark and the ship anchored at sea seemed like a distant dream. He wanted to go back to that dream and get out of this weird nightmare.

A pressure was building inside Landon's chest, and finally, he had to say something. "All these bones, Griggs. They *killed* all these animals?"

Griggs kept moving, his frail form draped in rags appearing almost ghostlike itself. They reached another opening, and Landon feared he would pass out from the fumes. But this stench—nasty as it was—carried some hope with it. Landon could tell that behind the smell were some animals—some *living* animals. He was a bit afraid to learn what kind of shape they were in, however. *At least they're still alive.*

They stepped inside the tunnel, and Landon's eyes adjusted

to a new darkness. A soft reddish glow seemed to come from nowhere but permeated everywhere. It was like viewing a scene through infrared lenses. Along either side, the ground continued on two level paths. Directly ahead of them, however, it sloped down in a wide ramp.

"There are seven tiers to the keep—this dungeon," Griggs explained. "This is the top tier." He stretched out his hands and then lowered them toward the ramp. "It goes down from here."

Hardy and Wagglewhip scanned their surroundings. Melech said, "Animals are living here. This is where they have. . .existed. . .since they were brought here. It smells very unhealthy. This is where they wanted to take me."

Although he said *they,* everyone knew Ludo and Wagglewhip had been involved.

"I didn't know," Wagglewhip whimpered. "I didn't. . .I didn't understand. . . ."

Landon feared the poor fellow was about to start bawling. But he only sniffled and shook his shoulders.

"I am not blaming you," said Melech. The horse stood near Wagglewhip and nuzzled his shoulder. "I am only observing and contemplating."

"Let's get dese aminals out of here," said Hardy. He glanced eagerly at Griggs and Dot, and then he cast his eye on Landon. "So, what do we do?"

Landon shriveled. "I—I don't—"

Dot had been very quiet, but now she interrupted. "Look at these," she said. She was kneeling and lowering the hem of her dirty patchwork tunic where, apparently, she had collected some small bones. Landon couldn't help cringing at the sight of each tiny bone as she laid it carefully on the ground. But then he found himself leaning over with interest as she set the bones into patterns. She was forming the shapes of animals.

Dot pointed. "A bat, a fish, a snake, a bird, and a lizard." She sat back on her haunches as if pondering something. Then she reached forward to touch one bone, drawing her finger along it and then looking at her finger. "These bones appear almost burned."

Everyone looked at her. Landon could sense the darkness swirling behind him, the fire occasionally blinking blue. The Arcans were out there. *That was them.* Yet they seemed so intent on the fire and what they were doing with it that Landon thought they might not notice anything going on along their periphery. Even the shadows seemed to be ignoring this party of intruders. Something curious must be going on down there.

"Almost burned?" asked Griggs. He crouched beside his wife, and the couple formed a picture of two cavemen surveying the remnants of their dinner.

Gross, Landon thought, trying to erase the image from his mind.

"Yes," said Dot. "Almost burned. It's like they'd been thrown into the fire and. . .and exploded or something. How else would their bones become scattered along the rim?"

"What sort of arcane alchemy are they up to, anyway?" Griggs wondered aloud.

A shriek sounded from behind them, accompanied by a burst of blue light. The noise sent shivers down Landon's spine like the screech of fingernails along a chalkboard. As his skin prickled from the noise, it came again, a wail unlike anything he'd ever heard. Beneath the high-pitched scream, however, he also heard a deep rumbling growl. What sort of creature could possibly make such a noise?

Landon trembled.

Dot and Griggs stood, scattering the bones. "Come on," said Griggs. He walked along the left ledge and paused at the first opening. The others gathered and peered in. Five sets of eyes glared back at them. The eyes glowed with a dull red light.

"They're. . .they're bears," said Landon, discerning the hulking shapes of the animals around their eerily glowing eyes. "They look awful."

"They're extremely malnourished and not only from lack of food," said Dot sadly. "As Melech said, the animals have merely existed here in the dungeon. No fresh air, no sunlight, no exercise. It's a miracle most of them are still alive."

And it's going to take a miracle to get them out of here, thought Landon, looking at the pathetically passive beasts. The bears' breathing came in slow, rough, rasping sounds. One bear took a lumbering step sideways. Much of its apparent bulk was only sagging skin and fur with nothing to fill it out. Would these creatures have the strength to get out of their pen?

It seemed everyone was sensing the hopelessness of the situation. Landon felt his own strength draining away. Griggs and Dot were right. Even though they could get to the animals, there was no way they could ever get them out of here.

"The rest aren't any better off," said Griggs. "I'm sorry."

"Not your fault," said Hardy. He patted Griggs between his bony shoulder blades. "Well," he sighed, "we tried."

Landon wanted to cry. Even though Hardy hadn't looked his way, he could guess what he was thinking. *You had de vision, young Landon. We were counting on you.* But it wasn't Landon's fault. He had never asked for a vision, and he had told Hardy it hadn't made any sense to him. So he'd "seen" animals at a football game. So what? He did not want to be held responsible for this failed mission.

Instead of crying or blaming Hardy or Vates or anyone else, however, Landon took a deep breath (which nearly made him gag), closed his eyes, and lifted his face to the ceiling of the cave. One word formed in his mind and heart and fled upward from his soul.

Help.

The shriek sounded from the pit. It was followed by a loud, breathy hiss. *"Intrudersss."*

Without a word, Griggs clambered toward a wall and began tearing off sheets of moss. "Protect your ears!" Griggs's voice echoed down the dungeon. "The curse is coming!"

Griggs handed out pieces of moss as people came running over. Landon took two sections and was scrambling to roll them into balls when, from out of nowhere, a small animal came leaping at him.

"Look out!" someone shouted, too late.

The creature latched onto Landon's stomach. Without thinking, Landon madly clutched at it, trying in vain to rip it away. But the animal was relentless. As Landon swung this way and that, he wrestled himself right down to the ground. Tiny claws dug into his uniform. In Landon's hands, the thing now felt like a furry, panting ball. Onto his back Landon rolled with it. Cold sweat ran down his face. Finally, Landon let his hands drop to his sides along the ground. His chest heaved as the bundled animal clung to his belly.

"Plug your ears. . .now!"

The voice came so loudly, Landon knew Griggs had already jammed his ears with moss.

The back of Landon's head began to throb. His mind began to swim. He blindly groped the hard, gritty surface around him. Where were his moss pieces?

From outside came a deep *thrum—thrum, thrum.* The earth itself seemed to be humming. Landon knew it was the Arcans.

He noticed something else. *They're stomping,* Landon realized, feeling the tingle on the back of his head. The Arcans were tamping the bottom of the pit with their feet in rhythm. Stamping and humming. Chanting and marching. Landon could picture their lanky arms raised around the fire as their throats pulsed with the ghastly, guttural note.

In the middle of the fire stood one Arcan, taller than the rest. An animal skull rested atop his head, the skull's eyes glowing red while the Arcan's dull, black eyes seemed to emit only darkness. *Shadow eyes,* thought Landon. *Eyes of a shadow that seeks only darkness, not light.* The animal skull was framed by two horns projecting outward and curving forward to sharp points.

It was the Arcan chief, Landon knew. *Chief Arcanum.* Was this really happening out there in the pit? Or was Landon only seeing it in his mind's eye? *I'm seeing a vision,* he thought, *but it seems real.* It was like he was in two places at once.

The chief raised his arms, and the humming and stamping

stopped. In the silence that followed, Landon imagined hundreds of red eyes, thousands of them, staring dully from the cavelike cells in the keep. The animals were waiting. They hungered to hear the curse—this curse that held them in their state of living death.

This place stinks, Landon thought.

The creature squirmed against his stomach. It almost tickled.

The world seemed to stand still, waiting.

The chief raised his head, looking up into the swirling funnel of shadows.

Another picture came into Landon's mind. He was back on the ship, looking at the island from afar. A column of smoke rose from the island. *Not smoke,* Hardy had said, *shadows.*

It all came to Landon. The sights, the sounds, the smells—everything about this island was *evil.* It was as if the island itself was a manifestation of Malus Quidam. *He's everywhere,* thought Landon.

The prince of darkness is too big for just one fight. So we have to keep fighting.

With the Auctor's help. . .

Something like a grin formed on the chief's drawn face, although it held no joy. The flames themselves, which had been writhing and dancing, shot straight upward. The tornado slowed to a crawl of circling black wraiths. Complete silence reigned. The prelude to the curse.

Landon tried to sit up, but he felt pinned to the ground by some strange force. He flailed his arms like he was making a snow angel. Where were the earplugs?

At the last moment, he gave up and hugged the ball of fur

against his belly. Landon didn't think about plugging his ears with his fingers until it was too late. The humming had stopped, and now a voice was calling out the strange and mysterious words of the curse.

"Icky—la boom bah!"

The words rang throughout the tunnel, echoing from the depths of the keep.

"Icky—la picky wicky!"

Landon trembled. He grasped the furry creature to himself as tightly as it clutched at his uniform. With his eyes squeezed shut—as if that might help ward off the curse—a strange thought kept recurring in Landon's brain. *Don't let go—I won't let go—I will never let go—*

"Uffa—la guffa wuffa!"

A convulsion ran through his body.

Landon thought of his family. He pictured his mom and dad, Holly and Bridget. He imagined them gathered around the table at Grandma Alice and Grandpa Karl's house, eating one of Grandma's famous meals. Then they'd retire to the living room where Grandpa would regale them with a story. The fire would blaze in the fireplace. A log would break and fall, sending up a shower of sparks. . .*gish!*

"Ooka-tee-ahh. . ."

The breathy *ahh* sound continued ringing throughout the caverns, like ocean sounds in a giant seashell.

"Ahhh—"

Landon wondered when it would stop, if it would stop.

"Ahhh—"

But part of him didn't want it to stop, because when the last sound of the curse ceased, then it would be over. He would die. *My ears are unplugged.*

Landon's heart clenched as he realized something—his *mouth* was unplugged, too. That is, his mouth was open wide, and sound was coming out from it.

He sat up, holding the animal.

"Ahhh—"

Finally, Landon closed his mouth. A moment later, the whispering echo faded. Faintness overcame Landon. He'd been so tense throughout the curse that he now felt completely spent. The creature relaxed, loosening its death grip. Landon lifted it above him, holding it out at arms' length, where it hung loosely in his hands. Previously, Landon had wondered if it might be a small cat. This was no cat. Finding his voice, Landon croaked, "You're a ferret."

The ferret's red eyes had turned a warm, amber hue. They still glowed, as if caught in the beam of a flashlight. Glancing past the ferret, Landon noticed the entire dungeon radiated like honey.

"What is going on?" Landon pondered aloud. In awe, he remarked, "I'm still alive."

Hardy, Wagglewhip, and the others were shuffling closer from behind. They stood on either side of Landon as they pulled clumps of moss from their ears. Griggs knelt beside him.

"How—*how* did you *do* that?" The skinny man's eyes were wide with wonder.

"He had de vision." It was Hardy. He snorted. "Vates knew he did. Dat your vision would save us."

"It wasn't so much the *vision*," said Landon. "I think I just called an audible."

The others looked at him, bewildered.

Landon smiled. "It's a football term." Griggs and Dot stared at his feet. "What I mean is, the Auctor had told me those words or sounds. He had called in the play on the football field that day." Landon gazed at the passively limp ferret. "I didn't fumble. But"—he looked questioningly at Griggs—"what was I saying?"

Dot replied, staring down at him. "You must have spoken the curse." Her eyes fluttered to the ferret. "Look at it. It's so calm."

With a gasp, Dot grabbed her husband's shoulder. "Buttercake, it's—it's Feister!"

Griggs squeaked almost like a rubber toy, and then he arose. "Your brother's pet?"

Dot nodded. Suddenly somber, she said, "Ludo."

The ferret had perked up at the sound of its name. Now it seemed to be looking or sniffing for its former master.

"Feister," said Landon, thinking of another happy reunion on the beach. "Oh, he'll be glad to see you!"

Where was the yellow light coming from? Landon could see it in Feister's eyes and now in other pairs of eyes that emerged along the paths before him. The light wasn't coming *from* the animals' eyes; it seemed to be reflecting some invisible source.

He's here, Landon thought, looking up toward the jagged ceiling as a thrill ran through him. *The Auctor.*

Animals continued to appear from their dens—crawling, hopping, waddling, lumbering, padding—each stepping slowly as if still waking from a deep sleep. Gradually, they began testing their voices, and the cave came alive with the sounds of a thousand animals.

"They're all looking at us," said Landon, stunned by the sight of so many eyes coming their way.

"They're looking at *you*," corrected Wagglewhip. "You have spoken the curse, and so broken it. And it seems you have reversed it, as well. The animals will now follow you. They'll listen to *your* voice, not Chief Arcanum's."

Landon set Feister down. As Landon stood, however, the ferret scampered right up his leg and lodged itself on his left shoulder. The ferret's nose sniffed in Landon's ear, and Landon giggled despite himself.

"What do I do?" asked Landon. Before, he carried the burden of having seen "de vision" and so felt responsible for the success or failure of this mission. Now he had a forestful of animals looking to him. "What do I say?"

Melech stepped forward. His strong, sure presence put Landon at ease—a little.

"How about telling them that they are free? And that they are to follow you back to their home in Wonderwood?"

Some deer were cautiously climbing the ramp from a level below. A horde of squirrels followed.

Landon gulped and then took a deep breath. "Animals of Wonderwood," he announced, waiting for the animals to quiet. "The curse is broken! You are free!"

Feister zipped from his left shoulder to his right and then back again, circling Landon's neck in tiny claws and fur. "Now follow me! We're taking you home!" His last word echoed into silence.

The animals seemed to be listening, but they gave no reaction. Landon wondered how on earth they were all going to make it back round the rim of the pit to the main tunnel.

"What's wrong?" Landon whispered toward Griggs. "They don't seem to understand."

"Perhaps you need a translator?" said Griggs.

"Come on!" Hardy shouted. "Aminals! Follow us!" Hardy turned, raised one sword, and charged toward the entryway. Halfway there, however, he stopped and looked back. No one had moved.

A blue flash turned Hardy's sword-brandishing figure into a stark silhouette against the opening of the keep. A high-pitched shriek followed, accompanied by an unnatural rumble from outside. Out of the corner of his eye, Landon saw Feister's eyes momentarily show red before resuming their friendly yellow glow. Landon's neck hair was standing on end.

"What can we do?" Landon asked himself. "How can we get these animals out of here?"

"Intruders!" The bellow came from outside, followed by a great, bloodcurdling shout. The Arcans were surely approaching the keep from below.

Melech stepped forward and neighed. After clopping his

hoof several times, he neighed again. The animals became rapt. After a beat of silence, the cavern filled with a deafening cacophony of chattering and growling and roaring and howling. Then the animals began moving forward as one.

"What did you say?" asked Landon as he unconsciously began backing toward the entrance.

Melech was retreating, too, with purposeful, high-leg-lifting clops. "I communicated that they are free, and that they should follow you."

"Is that all?" The animals' advance seemed particularly excited to Landon. The glow in their eyes had taken on a new intensity.

"And that there is food for them on the beach."

"Well, there is—although it is actually on the ark." Melech was nodding vigorously as if he were performing some sort of dance.

The shouting from outside grew louder. Hardy had kept his sword out and was now peering down from the entrance. "Dey're getting close! And dere are too many!"

Something swooped into the cavern over Hardy's head, and Landon thought a stray arrow had somehow bounced inside. He ducked as the object flew over his own head. Whatever it was, it was alive. Landon's heart leapt when he heard the familiar call.

"Twee-too! Twee-too!"

The bird dropped over the ramp of animals and disappeared below, its chirp fading.

A few moments later, with a great fluttering *whoosh*, a thousand birds arose from the depths of the dungeon. The air was filled with their flapping. And the music—it was like the tinkling of a thousand wind chimes amid the trills of flutes and piccolos. As the massive wave of birds flew out of the cave like bubbles from a bottle tipped underwater, Landon heard the call of the final bird as it passed stealthily overhead. "Hoo! Hoo!"

"Go, owl!"

At least the birds were free. As swiftly as they had flown up, however, they now swished downward past the opening, their calls and songs turned to battle cries.

"Thanks, Epops!" Landon shouted. Turning to Melech, he said, "We have air support."

But how long could the birds hold off the Arcans?

A bear approached Melech, stood on its hind legs, and draped an arm over Melech's neck. The two looked like old friends. The bear's head tilted toward Melech, and the bear let out a low growl. Melech's ears pricked, and then he nodded. The bear fell to all fours and lumbered toward its stall. Once inside, it rose again, and the other four bears joined it, rising and then turning their backs to the cavern.

Landon patted Melech's neck. "What was *that* about? Why are they going back into their cave? Are they giving up?"

"They want us to follow them," said Melech. "All of us. The animals, too."

"But—"

Landon felt his jaw drop open. The dark shapes of the bears matched the vision he'd had at the game. *The offensive linemen.* They were standing, facing away from him, pawing at something. Compelled by the strange scene, Landon took several steps closer. On either side of him, two inky figures slipped by. Landon felt the wind from their movement. *Shadows don't cause wind, do they?* The dark creatures disappeared behind the waving forms of the bears. What was going on here? Then they reappeared, one darting through two bears and the other coming around the right end. Landon froze. He was gaping at a panther and a wolf.

Just like in my vision.

But he had little time to think and no time to move. Somehow, the wolf reached him first, lunging at him with outstretched forepaws. It seemed like slow motion seeing the big, broad head with fuzzy, pointed ears zooming in. But Landon knew it happened in an instant. Then he lay flat on his back, the great beast pinning him to the ground.

This isn't Jake Adams, Landon thought as his head began to throb. *It's a real wolf this time.* The wolf narrowed its yellow eyes. With bared teeth, it thrust its head toward Landon.

Landon's life did not flash before his eyes. One thought did occur to him. *The wolf is smiling.* Well, of course it was. Landon was probably the poor creature's first real meal in a long time. What wolf wouldn't smile at the thought of eating a healthy young boy?

Landon shut his eyes and turned away. The wolf's heavy breath warmed his cheek, and then Landon felt something wet and leathery sliding along his skin. He heard a slurping sound, and he tried not to scream.

Landon waited, every muscle taut. He could feel a cool stripe on his cheek tingling in the musty air. The pressure had been released from his upper arms. Slowly, he opened his eyes, and then he turned his head.

The wolf was gone.

Landon sat up, his heart still hammering. "Where'd it go?"

"Back to his pack, I presume," said Melech. "That was Ravusmane. He wanted to say thank you."

Landon rubbed the back of his head. Then he touched the drool on his cheek and grimaced. "I've been *licked.*" Melech snorted—was he laughing? "Well," said Landon, "he's welcome, I guess." Welcome for what, Landon wasn't fully sure. They were still inside the keep, and it seemed they might be trapped. Landon looked around. Where had the panther gone? The black cat seemed to have vanished as swiftly and silently as it had appeared.

The bears continued to wave their forepaws, growling. What on earth were they doing? Landon feared they might be going mad.

Wagglewhip appeared, stepping alongside the leftmost bear. His sword drawn, Wagglewhip thrust it into the back of the cave. Was everyone going mad here? It occurred to Landon that it would be difficult to stay sane in a place such as this. How had Dot and Griggs survived?

Hope, they had said. He was the answer to their hope.

"Not me," Landon said softly. He glanced upward. *Help! You are the answer to our—*

Something happened. The back of the bears' den was crumbling. The bears had been digging at the wall, and it was falling down before them in a heap of rock and dirt. The bears fell to all fours and began clearing away the rubble, grunting. A breeze blew past Landon's face. The wet strip on his cheek tingled in the fresh air.

Dot stood nearby. "The bears had hope, too, it seems." She smiled at Landon and pointed. "That's another way out!"

Landon gulped hungrily at the air. Fresh air! With a hint of salt in it.

Shafts of light shone in the bears' revealed tunnel like glowing stripes. Landon thought of the opening they'd passed on the beach. It, too, had been strangely lighted. This had to be it. The bears had broken through the dead end from the inside!

Glancing to his right, Landon noticed a rolled-up ball of fur on the ground. "Feister"—he gently prodded it—"Feister?"

The ferret lifted its head, slightly dazed.

"Come on," said Landon. "It's time to run!"

Feister jumped into Landon's arms as he stood. But then, Landon bent partway over and lightly gripped his right thigh while cradling the ferret in his left arm.

"Blue twenty-two, blue twenty-two," said Landon. "Hut. . . hut—hut-hut!"

The bears rose onto their hind legs, parting to the left of center. Landon charged through the gap, never more determined to reach the end zone, which, in this case, meant the beach.

How many animals were charging behind him? It was hard to tell. Landon kept running, his sheathed sword banging against his leg. His lungs began to burn, but it didn't matter. Adrenaline was pumping through his limbs, propelling him on like a piston. Something told him to not look back, to just keep running and running. *And the animals will all follow me—to freedom!*

Hoofbeats gained on him. *Melech.* For an instant, Landon feared the horse was going to scoop him up from behind and fling him onto his back. But then Melech's head appeared, bobbing alongside. Landon smiled inside, straining ahead.

To his other side, something else was moving. With barely

a glance, Landon caught sight of a heaving, slinking shadow. *Except it's real. It's the black panther!* The realization made Landon gasp. It was an awesome sight. So stealthy and fast.

The intermittent shafts of light were giving way to a broader brightness ahead. Landon could faintly hear the pounding of the surf along the shore—a sound he hadn't even noticed when he was on the beach before. Probably because he'd grown accustomed to the waves while he'd been at sea for so long. Now the thumps and intermittent hushes were music to his hears.

And the smell! For two long strides, Landon closed his eyes to focus on the smell. The rankness of the animal keep had drifted behind. A fresh, briny breeze now filled his nostrils.

When Landon opened his eyes, two more figures were running alongside him. Griggs and Dot were so skinny—they looked so *weak*—Landon wished he had thought earlier to put them on Melech's back for the ride. But as he glanced at them, they were loping jubilantly, pacing as easily as conditioned marathon runners. Oh, the expressions lighting their faces! Landon had never seen so much anticipation, so much *hope*. Besides freedom and the sea and fresh air, Landon realized their long-lost daughter was waiting out there.

Ditty!

Landon's heart was now burning between his lungs. As his passion and determination drove him into another, higher gear, he felt streaks of liquid wetting his face like twin waterfalls. Sending up a silent thank you to the Auctor, Landon slowed his pace only after the rock ceiling vanished above him and the rocky floor gave way to spongy sand.

As light as the tunnel had been, the complete and sudden

brightness outside was overwhelming. Landon squinted, raising an arm against the glare. The beach shimmered like a desert. When his eyes finally adjusted, Landon peered toward the shore.

His friends and his sisters were not cheering or running to greet him. Behind them loomed a row of figures with black, gaping eyes. Animal skulls crested their elongated heads. In the middle stood one taller than the rest with a skull boasting long, outstretched horns that curved forward to sharp points.

Chief Arcanum.

Landon's first thought was for all the animals behind him to retreat back into the cave. But it was too late. They were spilling out onto the beach in droves. The stampede was reaching its end, and their collective heavy breathing drowned out even the sound of the waves, which appeared to silently curl and turn white and then collapse behind the Arcan line.

Had Dot and Griggs spotted their daughter? And had Ditty spotted them? Would she even recognize them? Landon wondered. For the moment, except for the panting, everyone remained still. Then a voice called out. "Landon!"

"Shat ap!" An Arcan shoved Bridget from behind, and she stumbled and fell onto the sand.

Landon's heart clenched into a ball. A new type of heat rushed through his veins. It took everything in him to keep from drawing his sword and charging. *That might not be the best idea,* he thought. What exactly were they dealing with here?

The horned Arcan pushed Vates and Ditty aside as he

strode forward. Halfway between the group on the shore and those near the rock, he stopped. Slowly, his head turned from the left to the right. His head seemed to move apart from his body, which remained eerily still. When his gaze passed across Landon's, Landon felt a cold stroke along his back like someone had run an ice cube over it. He unwittingly gasped. Though the Arcan's gaze had moved on, Landon still held his breath.

It wasn't the eyes that saw me, Landon thought with horror. *At least not the Arcan's eyes. It was the eyes in the skull.*

Indeed, the Arcan's eyes—though not empty sockets—appeared to be glossy, lifeless orbs. Almost like large black marbles. The eyes in the animal skull, however, contained tiny red dots. They appeared only for an instant, like lasers you can't see without looking directly into their source.

Weakness suddenly grabbed at Landon's knees with the force of a smashing crowbar. It felt like he was rocking, though somehow he managed to stay on his feet. He looked at Bridget still kneeling on the sand. Vates, Ditty, Holly—where was Ludo? Landon squinted toward the opening in the ark. It was dark. But was that the top of a head sticking out from one side?

Then Landon noticed something else. Beyond the ark, between the black cliffs that guarded the entrance to this harbor, a ship was sailing in. *Hoist the mainsail and lower the jib,* thought Landon. *Battleroot, you sly dog.* Landon warily glanced at the Arcan chief, hoping he hadn't caught Landon's gaze. *Don't turn around,* Landon willed. *No one turn around.*

The very next moment, however, Landon was wondering what good Battleroot could do them from the ship, anyway.

And the moment after that, Landon's heart really started to sink. *What if they capture all of us—which it seems they already have—and take the ark, and now our ship with Battleroot, too? We won't have anything left. Our last hope of escape will be gone.*

"Turn around," Landon found himself whispering. "Battleroot, turn around and get out of here!"

"Who leads these intruders and thieves?" asked the chief.

Perhaps it was his knees finally giving way, or perhaps it was the sense of responsibility he'd been carrying for this entire mission. Either way, Landon found himself feebly stepping forward. He was about to say, "I do," when he saw two others had stepped forward, as well. To his right stood Melech, and to his left stood Hardy. Landon had never felt so proud and humbled in his life. He was also quite grateful for the company.

Before any of the three had spoken, out jumped someone else bounding two more steps ahead. Open-mouthed, Landon watched as Wagglewhip raised and then lowered his sword, laying it down on the sand. A fresh set of tears dribbled down Landon's cheeks. *Wagglewhip, don't—*

The chief strode forward and with startling swiftness kicked Wagglewhip's sword straight up into the air and snatched it. His kick also sent a shower of sand over the humble figure before him.

"How did you steal my curse?" the chief bellowed. "How—"

Wagglewhip thrust out his arm, revealing his tattoo. Nothing in the chief's body seemed to react, but Landon was quite sure he'd noticed a red glimmer inside the animal skull on his head. It was like someone poking embers with a stick.

"You're. . .a. . .traitor." The chief snarled. His lips curled back—*like an animal's,* thought Landon—revealing teeth that looked more pointed and sharper than any human's. "But at least you confess." The *s* sound lingered and then abruptly stopped.

With another quick movement, the chief spun Wagglewhip around and drew the sword across his neck but didn't cut. Landon could sense the breathlessness around him. It was like standing inside a vacuum. Some of the animals behind him, the smaller ones, had begun to whimper. It seemed only a matter of time before they would all be slinking back into the dungeon.

Why was he feeling like this, Landon suddenly wondered. With the animals, his party greatly outnumbered the Arcans before them. Yet they already seemed defeated. It was as if something greater than the Arcans themselves was present here.

Yesss, a voice seemed to whisper. *It is I, Malus Quidam. And now surely you will die!*

Landon could hardly stand it. But the oppressive darkness was seeping into his soul. His adrenaline, all the energy that had propelled him this far, was entirely drained. The thought of laying down his sword and even laying down himself seemed utterly appealing. *I'll bet the sand is soft. It will feel good to lie down. I feel so tired.*

The Arcans stirred as their chief dragged Wagglewhip back toward their ranks. Vates, Ditty, Holly, and Bridget were prodded forward by the butts of the Arcans' swords. At first, Landon's heart leapt as his sisters and friends were forced to reunite with them. Bridget reached him first, clasping onto his leg like a miniature tackler. Holly embraced him, whispering something he couldn't discern. And then Ditty hugged him, though Landon was unable to return her embrace. He was starting to feel nauseous and dizzy. Something was not right about this. What was going on?

A pained woman's voice cried, "Ditty?"

Landon felt like he was spying on a private moment, but he couldn't help watching. He glanced at Griggs and Dot first, but then he kept his eyes on Ditty as she looked at her parents. Her expression changed from startled bewilderment to a scrutinizing stare. After eyeing each of them up and down, Ditty took a halting step toward them, searching their eyes with her own. Suddenly, something seemed to melt inside her.

"Mom?" she said, sounding out the unfamiliar word. "Dad?"

Ditty's eyes teared up, and then so did Landon's. He looked down, dripping tears into the sand.

"Now!"

Chief Arcanum had raised Wagglewhip's sword. The Arcan's other long arm wrung his victim's neck like a noose. "Now my little traitor, you will watch your worthless followers die."

Wagglewhip's eyes flared, and he struggled against the chief's grip. This only seemed to aggravate his captor, who merely tightened his hold. Eventually, Wagglewhip ceased to resist, drooping like a lifeless rabbit.

The other Arcans approached from either side of their chief, drawing their swords. *Were those swords from Wonderwood? How awful to die by their own swords.*

Growls and snarls came from behind him, and Landon felt his own hackles prickling. He felt, and he sensed the animals did too, that they were cornered. Even with their larger numbers, they were frail and exhausted. The Arcans didn't seem to feed on food; they fed on fear.

Landon felt a rumbling in his belly. A sympathetic hunger pang? The rumbling rose into his throat. He opened his mouth and growled. What was happening to him?

Something caught his eye beyond the advancing Arcans. A figure had stepped fully into view in the ark's doorway. *Ludo!* But what could he do? What did it matter now? The grumbling in Landon's stomach churned with bile. If it wasn't for Ludo, the animals never would have been sent here. It was all Ludo's fault!

Yesss, the voice hissed. *Hate him. Haaate hhhiii—*

The voice cut off. Something had happened. A commotion stirred among the animals, and the line of Arcans broke apart as a tiny creature darted toward them. Scampering right between two of them, the small animal continued to zip across the sand almost like a stone skipping over the water. It raced past the chief holding Wagglewhip and bounded up the ramp. The courageous critter leaped into Ludo's arms, sending both of them into the darkness of the ark before Landon realized what had happened.

"Feister," he said. "Feister!" The sound of his own voice shook Landon back to his senses. That was one animal aboard the ark, he thought, only a few thousand or so more to go!
We need your help, he prayed. Glancing at Ditty and her parents—*the Willowbranch family*—he saw they were already kneeling together with their heads bowed. From seemingly nowhere, Landon felt strength flowing into his legs, his arms, and his hands. They would not give up without a fight.

"I had de vision," said Landon softly.

Melech neighed on his right, and from his left came Hardy's cheering voice. "You did have de vision, Landon Snow. Dat you did."

Vates also stood nearby. Despite his apparent weariness, he slowly nodded and smiled at each of them.

"Look!" It was Bridget. "The ship's turned sideways."

Indeed it had, and the ship had sailed deeper into the harbor since Landon had noticed it before. What was Battleroot doing out there?

A bright flash from the ship's side seemed to offer an answer. And the boom that followed a second later confirmed it.

Landon hadn't heard a flying missile before. As he listened to a whistle dropping in pitch and growing louder, however, he instinctively reacted.

"Hit the deck!"

The next moment, an explosion shook the ground beneath him. Sand and bits of seashells rained down for several seconds. With his ears ringing, Landon looked up. He spit dirt from his mouth and had to wipe sticky debris from his face. The ark appeared huge and alone in the harbor. Its open doorway at the top of the ramp waited invitingly. Was it time to make a run for it? Would the animals all be able to get aboard?

But like camouflaged creatures rising from the beach, the Arcans stood again. Sand coated their bodies from head to foot, dribbling off as they resumed their inland march. One Arcan appeared to have two skulls on his head. Then he knocked one of them off, and Landon saw that it was a shell.

"Battleroot always did like dem dunder shooters."

Hardy's eyes peered at Landon from a mask of sand. One eye winked, spilling sand from his eyebrow. Landon smiled.

"Looks like he got two of them," said Landon scanning the line of Arcans. Indeed, there was a gap in their row, two bodies wide.

"And he got us, too." Melech snorted and shook his body like a wet dog.

"Hey!" said Landon blinking against the flying grains. "One beach shower was enough."

"Quick plan," said Hardy rising into a crouch. "Objective is de ark. Hey, horsey, you and me can shoot de gap and get some of dem turned around. Landon, when de pad is clear, lead de aminals drough."

"What about Wagglewhip?" asked Landon. Chief Arcanum was dragging the hapless fellow toward the ark's ramp. Soon he would be blocking their way.

Hardy half bowed his head. "He knew what dis mission was about more dan anyone. He's doing what he needs to do. Come, horsey."

Melech stepped out front, and Hardy clambered on. Before Landon could tell them to wait, the pair took off down the beach, kicking up sand. Hardy drew both of his swords, their blades glinting in the sun like shiny wings. One Arcan raised his sword with both hands, turning toward the horse and rider. With a swiftness Landon hardly thought possible, Hardy swung one sword clean through the Arcan's long chest. In a sight Landon would never forget, the Arcan fell like a sheaf of sand, his sword and animal skull dropping on top of him.

"Did you see that?" said Holly. "He disappeared!"

As she spoke, a wisp of black smoke arose from where the Arcan had fallen.

"They're not human," said Landon staring. *They're not human.*

He gripped his sword and slowly stood. "Holly—"

"I'm here," she said standing beside him.

"You may need to use your sw—"

"I can lift it, Landon, to kill one of those things."

They're not human.

What sort of arcane alchemy was this?

Arcane.

Alchemy.

I need to look those words up.

"Bridget."

"Yes?"

"Stay with the bears." Landon gave his youngest sister a warning look. With a nod at the five brown bears, he added, "They're good blockers."

A *clink* and a *clang* rang in the air. Another Arcan had successfully engaged Hardy in swordplay. Others were closing in. To Landon's horror, he noticed the chief was nearly halfway up the gangway to the ark, Wagglewhip still helplessly in tow.

"Oh no," said Landon. "We can't let him get aboard the ark. Holly, I've got to go."

Without waiting for a reply, Landon clenched the hilt of his sword and charged down the beach. Enough commotion surrounded Hardy and Melech so that Landon made it all the way to the first plank of the ramp before he heard something behind him. Swinging around with his sword in the air, Landon felt the jolting blow of metal on metal before he saw the Arcan facing him. The glossy black eyes stared blankly down at him, nearly mesmerizing him. For a long, dazed moment, Landon stood with his left foot planted on the ramp and his right foot pressing into the damp sand. His sword hummed like a giant tuning fork, buzzing through his hands and arms. Paralyzed with fear, Landon watched as the strange figure brought his sword behind his head and began to swing it around. When the blade seemed poised to strike, a growling blur of gray leaped into the Arcan, barreling him sideways. The point of the blade swished by, scraping Landon's uniform.

I think I just peed my pants.

Ravusmane was leaping in and out, snapping at the befuddled Arcan. One loud growl directed Landon's way seemed to say, "Go!"

Landon swiveled around. The chief was two-thirds of the way up. Eerily, he was grinning. As Landon ascended the planks, he became acutely aware of the noises around him. Waves rolled and splashed and washed up on shore, then fizzled back into the bay. The wood of the boards squeaked and groaned under his weight. Sounds of battle came from behind him—swords clanking, animals snarling, Hardy yelling, Melech neighing, bodies scuffling, and every now and then that strange *poof* sound when an Arcan fell.

They're not human.

The chief Arcan waited for him.

He's not human.

Landon could hear his own breathing: in and out, in. . .out. As the Arcan opened his mouth wider than any jawbone should allow, Landon heard a faint hissing ahead of the whispery words.

"So *iss thisss* the real leader then?" He thrust Wagglewhip out with his fingers wrapped about his neck. Wagglewhip appeared unresponsive. Landon wondered if it was too late.

"No," said Landon. He stopped just short of where he guessed Chief Arcanum could reach with his sword.

The chief wagged his victim back and forth, causing Wagglewhip's head to flop from side to side. Poor Wagglewhip looked like a dummy gesturing "no" for his ventriloquist.

"Then who *isss,* I wonder. Are you?" The chief's sword flashed forward, hovering a few inches from Landon's face.

Landon took a step back, but only one. He took a long, deep breath. Then he slowly shook his head. "No."

Wagglewhip's head snapped to one shoulder.

"Then *whooo isss iiit*?" The Arcan's head turned as his mouth hung unnaturally open. He was moving like he had earlier on the beach, scanning the scene before him. He was looking for their leader.

Landon watched with morbid curiosity. It was almost as if he wasn't there. Yet he knew that if he made a move, the sword before him would react like lightning.

What was this thing called an Arcan? Landon was beginning to make a guess.

"You won't see our leader that way," said Landon patiently. "We don't see him that way either, even though he's all around us."

The hovering sword lowered a notch. The Arcan gazed directly at Landon. "What did you *sssay*?"

Yeah, Landon thought nervously. *What am I saying?* He

swallowed the dryness in his throat. Over the hammering of his heart, Landon raised his voice. "We follow the Auctor."

Time seemed to freeze. Even the surrounding noise faded. Landon could feel his heart beating—*bump, bump, bump*—inside his chest. Then in a rush of sensation, everything came crashing back. Landon had his sword out before him just in time to catch the smashing blade of Chief Arcanum. Wagglewhip was tossed aside like a rag doll, dully splashing into the surf.

"*Yooouuu* don't know what it *isss* to *fall,* leetle boy."

The Arcan's sword released and then came back. Landon switched his angle and prepared for the blow. As the impact jarred his footing, part of his mind wondered if he had heard correctly. Had the chief said *fall* or *follow*?

Each swipe sent Landon reeling backward. Yet amazingly, he was able to ward off this staccato attack. The Arcan was grinning, however. The corners of his mouth were continually drawing upward as if being pulled by invisible wires. Was the creature merely toying with him? Landon wondered. Sweat was streaming down Landon's face and soaking his body. His arms and legs were beginning to tremble.

"Now *I* will teach you to *falll*!"

The long blade rose high as a monolith. Instead of slicing straight downward, however, the Arcan swiveled it one way but then drew it swiftly around the other way. Landon could only hold his sword up and bow his head, bracing himself for certain death.

Landon never felt the blade strike his body. Instead, he heard a metallic *ping* and felt his sword tingle in his hands.

An arrow—shot clear through from behind—jutted from

the Arcan's chest. The arrowhead had struck Landon's sword.

"Bad form, I know, shooting one in the back. But I really had no choice you see—my friend was under attack!"

Landon's heart leapt at the sound of the familiar voice. "Ludo!"

The Arcan seemed to awaken at the mention of Ludo's name. The protruding arrow hardly seemed to faze him. He began to turn, emitting a fluttery hiss that made Landon's skin crawl. "Ludo. I *knooow yooouuu.*"

The peculiar paralysis was returning to Landon's limbs. He wanted to move—now was his chance—but his arms and legs felt heavy as sandbags.

"We entrusted you with gold. Why couldn't you do as you were *told*?"

We? Landon thought. *We?*

"I—I. . . ," Ludo stammered.

Chief Arcanum marched up the ramp.

Landon closed his eyes. *Help.* When he opened his eyes, he found his legs were moving. Quickly he ascended the ramp, stretching out his sword to tap the feathered arrow in Chief Arcanum's back. *He won't like that,* Landon thought.

Sure enough, the Arcan spun. His sword was flying. This time, Landon ducked, waving his own sword behind him before swinging with all his might. The sound was almost like ripping paper, only much louder and thicker and grainier. As his sword came back around and Landon steadied himself, he caught a clear view of the Arcan's form dissolving and then falling with a thud to the planks. The strangest part was seeing the animal skull, horns and all, drop onto the sand. Inside the eye sockets, twin dots of red light dimmed and went out as if they had been unplugged.

But that wasn't all. As soon as the lights vanished, out trickled three streams of blackness—*three shadows*—from the skull. The shadows glided over the wood and then launched into the air. At first, Landon thought they had disappeared. But one came back into view, a snakelike haze passing before him. Landon watched, transfixed, as two red dots appeared, looking at him, before turning and flying away.

This battle's not done, Landon Snow.

Was that his own thought, Landon wondered, or had the shadow just left him a parting message?

"I got three of them!" Holly was panting and sweating as she climbed the ramp. "The last one went down easily, like a sack of potatoes. Or sandbags actually. How many did you get?"

Landon spread the pile of sand in front of him with his foot. Cautiously he nudged one thick horn with his sword. No more shadows slipped out. It seemed empty. Dead.

"Well," Holly persisted, "how many?"

"Um, I think I got three of them," said Landon lifting the arrow and then letting it fall. "Three in one."

"Huh," said Holly. "Three-in-One."

Landon glanced at the ark's doorway, but Ludo was nowhere to be seen.

"Here comes Bridget," said Holly. "Bridget and the Five Bears. Sounds like a story, doesn't it?"

"Yeah," said Landon. He was trying to remember something, but his mind was still reeling from the fight and the appearance and disappearance of the shadows. *What was it?*

A spluttering gasp from below reminded him.

"Wagglewhip!" Gazing over the edge, Landon called down to him. "Are you all right? You're alive!"

Wagglewhip coughed repeatedly, which under the circumstances appeared to be a good sign. "Yeah," he finally rasped. His voice sounded terrible. "Yeah—*cough, cough*—alive." He raised his hand in a feeble gesture that Landon took to be a thumbs-up.

"Thank goodness," Landon muttered. "And, thank the Auctor."

Across the beach were spread mounds of sand like ski moguls, though they were already beginning to scatter and flatten from the wind. Near each mound lay a sword, and atop each mound rested the skull from some animal. A wave of relief passed through Landon, tinged by a touch of sadness. *We didn't save those animals,* he thought, *but we can save the rest of them.*

"Let's get them on board the ark. It's time to go home."

"Let's go!" shouted Holly toward the beach. "All aboard!"

The five bears came lumbering toward the ramp, and Landon almost burst out laughing. Bridget clung to the middle bear's shaggy back like a big burr caught on a dog. As the bears started up the ramp, Landon stepped in front of them, and they stopped.

"Off, Bridget," he said.

"Aw, Landon." Bridget nestled herself deeper into the fur, gazing up at her big brother with her most puppyish eyes.

"No, Bridget. You can't go with him. And no"—he raised his hand as she opened her mouth—"he can't come with us."

"But you told me to stay with him, with all of them."

Landon sighed, and he smiled. "Yes, back there for your protection. Not now, and not here. The bears are going home. And so, I hope, are we."

With one more "aw," Bridget reluctantly slid from the bear's back. She hugged each of the five bears. They gently growled in response before sauntering up the ramp to enter the ark. Or perhaps that had been their poor stomachs rumbling.

Holly had begun her counting, of course. Landon said there was another who could keep track of the animals—who should keep track of the animals again, he added. Then Landon went up the ramp to search for Ludo, pausing along the way to pick up Wagglewhip's sword and Ludo's arrow.

Holly and Bridget wanted a peek inside the ark, as well, of course. Who wouldn't want to see the interior of a massive, floating zoo? It was very long and tall, as they already knew. What astounded them was how *deep* the vessel was. The phrase that came into Landon's mind was "the tip of the iceberg." What they could see from the outside above the water was only a small portion of the full size of the ark. It was simply enormous. Bigger, Landon realized, than the animal keep, and with at least as many tiers. The animals' spaces were roomier and much more pleasant—some already bedded with hay, others with fresh dirt and grass, and still others with leaves. For the birds, Landon saw a variety of nesting materials, and tree limbs jutted in from the ark's wooden walls.

Landon and his sisters toured the full interior of the vessel. As they made their way back toward the ramp, Bridget suddenly pouted.

"I want to ride in here."

"Do you really?" Landon paused at the entrance, allowing his sister to make up her mind. "It would probably be best if we stuck together now. And I don't think this"—he indicated the ark—"will be going where we're supposed to go."

Bridget glanced at him. "Button Up?"

Landon nodded.

"Well," said Bridget sighing, "I'm sure going to miss all the animals."

"I will too," said Landon, putting his arm around her. "I think we all will."

Holly nodded and sharply turned away. Had that been a tear glistening in her eye?

A symphony of song filled the ark as the birds streamed in not only from the doorway but also through the high, rectangular windows. It was a wonderful foretaste of how the forest would sound in a few days. Part of Landon wanted to stay on this ship, too. Whereas only minutes earlier it had been an empty, lonely vessel, now it was fairly booming with life.

But where was Ludo?

Landon realized they hadn't climbed to the top deck and the pilothouse. *He's probably up there,* Landon decided. Perhaps it would take some time for Ludo to feel comfortable around all the animals again. Landon sensed the poor fellow still carried a load of guilt for having sent these animals away. *I'd feel badly, too,* Landon thought. It would be quite a burden to bear. *At least Feister's with him.* Feister had obviously been excited to see his old master again. The ferret would help ease Ludo back into the company of animals.

Along the beach, Landon noticed that the mounds of sand

from the fallen Arcans were gone. The sand was flat. The Arcans' swords had been picked up, as well. All that remained as a remnant of the battle were the scattered animal skulls. The skulls would soon be washed away by the rising tide. For now, however, they marked not the loss of the Arcans, but the loss of the animals to which they had previously belonged.

Ditty and her parents had crossed the beach and were making their way up the ramp. Ditty hugged each of Landon's sisters and then gazed at Landon. He looked back at her for a long time.

A breeze stirred Ditty's hair—lifting it and then letting it gently fall.

The wind's picking up, thought Landon. *It will be good for sailing.*

"So—you met my mom and dad then," said Ditty finally. She kept her voice steady, although Landon could sense a flood of emotion being held back. The corner of Ditty's mouth gave away a small twitch.

Landon felt his own throat tighten. "Yes."

Another breeze blew past. Strangely—or providentially—this time the wind seemed to tug at Landon from behind. Perhaps it was swirling through the cove and circling back out?

Ditty's hair had flown partially across her face. She brushed it back, and Landon thought she had secretly wiped away a tear with it. "Thank you," she said.

"You're wel—"

Ditty's squeeze cut short Landon's reply. It didn't matter. Words hardly seemed necessary. After shaking hands with Griggs and Dot, Landon gave Ditty one last, meaningful look before striding down the gangway. From behind, he could hear Griggs saying to his family, "That is one extraordinary young man."

"He is," came Ditty's voice. "He really is."

Vates was waiting on the beach with Hardy, Melech, and Wagglewhip, who appeared healthy although still shaken up. Vates looked more tired than usual. He was an old man, of course. But it had been a long time since Landon had thought of him that way.

"Well done, Landon," said Vates, leaning on his stick. "Well done, indeed. On behalf of all Wonderwood, I thank you and your sisters"—the old man nodded to them—"for your help."

"And though I was not imprisoned on this island myself, I believe I can speak for the animals who were." Melech's mane ruffled in the wind as he bowed his head. "Thank you, young Landon. You have done your duty, and we are all glad for it."

Though Landon appreciated everyone's gratitude, it was somewhat hard to accept. Receiving their thanks only reminded him of the responsibility he'd been carrying throughout this mission.

"The Auctor gave me the vision," said Landon. "I only did what seemed right in the moment. That's all."

"Exactly," said Vates, a glimmer returning to his eyes. "Exactly."

"I guess you're probably all going back to Wonderwood?" said Landon hesitantly. His resistance to expressing his emotions was crumbling. Thank goodness he'd already made it through saying good-bye to Ditty. This was getting to be too much.

Vates nodded and then said, "But Hardy and Wagglewhip will see you back to your ship and see that you get started safely on your way."

"I want to see Wonderwood," said Bridget sadly as she tugged on Landon's sleeve. "It's not fair."

Landon sighed and gave Vates a questioning look. Vates mysteriously narrowed his eyes, peering beyond Landon and the ark. Then his face softened and he refocused on Landon. "Not this time," he said, sounding tired. He held Landon with his gaze, and Landon could tell Vates was both here with them on the beach and thinking of something a world away.

"When?" asked Bridget, her voice rising excitedly.

"Yeah, when do we go back to Wonderwood?" chimed in Holly.

Landon squinted at Vates, trying to penetrate his distant thoughts. Seeing nothing himself, Landon raised his eyebrows as if to say, "Well?"

Vates came wholly back and smiled down at the girls. "In due time," he said nodding. "In due time."

From somewhere beyond the black cliffs of the cove arose a far-off cry. A tingling along Landon's spine told him he'd heard that shriek before, only much closer and accompanied by an eerie blue flash.

"It's time to depart this place," said Vates.

Landon agreed.

"What was that?" asked Holly, frowning up at the rock face.

"Some arcane alchemy," said Landon, pulling her and Bridget toward the jolly boat. "Come on!"

When his sisters were seated in the boat, Landon ran back to the bottom of the ramp and caught Vates. Landon gave him a hug, feeling the old man's tense frame soften in his grasp. When Landon ran back to his boat, he almost butted heads with Melech.

"Had to say farewell to the little misses," said Melech.

"Yes," said Landon, suddenly at a loss for words. He hugged Melech's neck for a long time. He could sense the horse's ears twitching.

"We have been through a lot together, you and I," said Melech. "And I dare say we may still see more adventures ahead."

Running his fingers through Melech's mane, Landon leaned back and studied his friend. "I like the sound of that. Indeed," he added, slightly choking, "I do like the sound of that."

Melech snorted and nodded. Was the staid horse fighting back emotion, too?

"Until next time then, young Landon." He turned away.

Something swelled inside Landon's chest. "Wait!"

Melech turned back, his ears alert. "Yes, young Landon?"

Inhaling deeply, Landon gazed up and down the stretch of sand. "How about a quick run on the beach? You know, uh, for old time's sake?"

Melech didn't move. "Old time's sake?"

"It's an expression." Landon grinned. "What do you say?" He cast a wary eye toward the rise of black rock. No blue flashes or strange screams—only blue sky and puffy white clouds.

"I say, let's go!"

His heart skipping with joy, Landon climbed onto Melech's back, and they set off at a gallop down the beach. As Melech's hooves pounded and splashed the surf beneath them, Landon tilted back his head and laughed. In the jolly boat, everyone cheered and clapped, while Vates leaned on his staff, shaking his head. Then the old prophet smiled, too, and his body rocked with laughter.

"Thanks, Melech. That was fun." Landon gave his friend a final hug and patted his neck.

Melech made a sputtering noise. "For old time's sake," he said. And if a horse could smile, well, then that's what he seemed to be doing.

Landon helped Hardy shove the boat from the sand into the surf. Wagglewhip was told to rest and not exert himself. In a numb sort of stupor, the poor fellow sat beside Bridget. She was doing her best to cheer him up.

Landon climbed aboard and turned to watch the ramp disappear into the ark. As Hardy started rowing, putting water between the boat and the beach, somehow the ark also became dislodged from the shore. It drifted sideways before beginning to slowly turn about.

"Oh yeah," said Landon, half facing Hardy, "I wanted to ask you. How did the ark move at sea when there wasn't any wind? I mean, how did you catch up to us? And just now"—Landon pointed at the hulking brown-and-gray vessel—"how did it do that?"

"Well," said Hardy between heaving grunts, "de tide's rising now, which helped some wid dat." He groaned, dipping and pulling the oars. "But earlier at sea—*ungh*—we had a one-horsey-power paddlewheel—benead de surface," he added as Landon gaped.

Landon could hardly contain himself. "You mean—are you saying that *Melech* propelled that thing all by himself?"

Though he was still grunting as he strained at the oars, it sounded like Hardy was smiling when he said with a hint of pride, "Dat is one strong horsey."

Landon laughed in amazement. "Incredible."

"Now they've got, well, a whole forestful of animals to help." Holly sounded a bit miffed at not knowing precisely how many animals were actually aboard the ark.

"Yeah," said Bridget in open-mouthed wonder, "they'll get home fast."

Chapter Twenty-One

Everyone remained thoughtfully quiet on the ride to the ship, even when Battleroot threw down the ropes and invited Hardy to help him hoist up the boat. Landon sat looking out at the water as the boat lurched into the air, swaying and occasionally bumping the ship's hull with a thud. Eventually, they found themselves back on board the ship. In some strange way, it felt like they had come home.

At least a step closer to home, he thought.

After loading the jolly boat with swords and other supplies, Hardy and Battleroot maneuvered it back out over the railing. When they had each leaped into it from the ship—Wagglewhip, too—Hardy instructed Landon and Holly to lower them down.

"Dat's it, dat's it. Steady. . .easy dere. . ."

Despite the heavy load, the pulley system made the job seem easy. Once the boat hit the water, Landon and Holly towed the ropes back up and swung the empty pulley over the deck.

"Heave ho, Landon Snow!" Hardy shouted above the waves. "And you, too, little misses!"

Wagglewhip and Battleroot waved with both hands. Wagglewhip seemed to be returning to his old self again.

Through his telescope, Landon watched the boat disappear inside the ark's ramp opening. Shortly thereafter, the giant, wing-like sails emerged on either side, and the ark began sailing swiftly ahead.

Before it got too far away, however, Landon caught sight of a figure on the top deck. Focusing in, he saw Ludo wearing a furry scarf around his neck. When the scarf stood and sniffed at the air, Landon laughed.

"Good-bye, Ludo," he muttered. "You, too, Feister."

Landon released one hand to wave, momentarily dropping the spyglass from Ludo. When Landon raised the scope again, Ludo and Feister were too small to distinguish. Landon was pretty sure, though, that he'd seen Ludo smile.

The ark itself soon receded in the distance, shrinking as it neared the horizon. All that was left was a greenish white wake on the surface of the sea.

The sky had turned pink and was gradually darkening toward red.

Sailors' delight.

At some point, Holly and Bridget had gone to the captain's quarters to prepare a meal after sending off the jolly boat.

"Lan—don!" Holly's voice called from the cabin's entryway. "Come here, please!"

Landon took a long, wistful look up at the crow's nest before passing beneath the barricade of sails. They were sailing along at a decent clip, too, though they didn't have any animal paddle-power to propel them. But they weren't really in any hurry—were they?

"Lan—"

"I'm coming!"

Landon paused to glimpse the bridge from below before reaching his sister. They had secured the helm with rope, tying down the middle pages for a straight course. But something was wrong. The rope had come undone, and the pages appeared to be flipping willy-nilly back and forth.

"Holly—"

Landon caught himself. Something *was* wrong, or at least very different. The ship was not veering in any direction in response to the pages' turning. The ship's course remained steady and true. The sails were billowed full out.

We're going exactly where we're supposed to be going, thought Landon.

It felt like he was waking from a dream. *No,* he thought, *it feels like I'm slipping into one.*

"What?" Holly stepped forward while craning her neck to look back up.

"Nothing," said Landon pushing her back inside. "Now what is it you wanted? Is everything okay? Is dinner ready? Where's Bridget?"

"I'm in here!" came his youngest sister's voice as he entered the cabin.

Landon swiveled to his left. Holly had already entered the cubbyhole. Her voice came next.

"We have all the oranges we could ever ask for—seventy-eight of them right here, if you must know—and these twenty-nine loaves of bread still look good, amazingly enough. But the ginger ale, Landon, it's—what's this?"

Landon stepped in behind her and felt the change.

Holly was holding a big plastic bottle of Coke.

Landon blinked.

The lighting was different. A single bulb—not too bright and not too dim—shone overhead.

The kids were back in their own clothes, not uniforms.

The ship wasn't moving, because—

"This is Grandma's pantry." Landon blinked, still taking it in. "We're back in Button Up."

A door opened behind him, and Landon jumped. He spun around. The sight of his mother was shocking.

"Ah!" She appeared startled herself. "For heaven's sake alive! Here you kids are. We've been looking all over for you. What is this, some kind of group hide-and-seek? Kids versus grown-ups? Landon, Holly, Bridget"—their mother leaned in, her eyes roving with suspicion or relief—"what on earth? And how did you sneak in here?"

"What? What happened? Where am I?" Bridget rubbed by Landon to go hug her mother. "Mom!"

A potent odor caught Landon's nose, and he recoiled. "What's that smell?" he asked warily.

"Well!" came Grandpa Karl's voice as he emerged from the dining room. "It's getting crowded in here, eh? You kids are just in time for supper. A special treat tonight—seafood!"

The kids stood still as statues. Something about Grandpa Karl's presence, however, helped put Landon at ease. At least a little bit.

"Oh," said Landon finally as he gave Holly a nudge. "Great."

"Yeah," said Holly, "sounds good."

Bridget made a noise somewhere between a whimper and a moan, but Holly thrust the Coke bottle into her little sister's hands. "Could you put this back, please, Bridget?" Holly flared her eyes and nodded deeply for emphasis.

"I was a little worried, you should know." Their mother let go of Bridget to place her hands on her hips. "All day down at the library? What were you three doing? I know you like to read"—she glared at Landon—"and you were probably counting things"—she said to Holly—"but you, Bridget?"

Bridget had one foot in the pantry and the other foot out. She held the Coke as if she'd just been caught stealing it.

"What were you doing?"

Bridget's mouth hung open, speechless.

Landon and Holly glanced at each other.

"She felt a little sick," said Landon suddenly, "after that long walk and all."

"Yeah," said Holly, "so she rested. Even fell asleep." She giggled nervously.

This wasn't lying, was it? Landon wondered. Thankfully, Grandpa Karl came to their rescue, and in more ways than one.

"I know you three didn't stay inside the BUL the whole time you were down there," he said, leaning in.

Landon gulped as he heard tiny gasps escape from his sisters.

Grandpa Karl brought out his hand, which had been behind his back. This time there was no helping it. Landon gasped aloud with Holly and Bridget. In their grandfather's large hand were both Holly's backpack and Landon's Bible. Landon took the heavy, old, worn book and fingered it tenderly. *It's not wet,* he thought with astonishment. *And it seems okay.* Meanwhile, Holly clutched her pack to her chest like a life jacket.

"That's right," said Grandpa Karl. Was he genuinely upset or was he only pretending? It was hard to tell. "I found those items in the lobby sitting right outside Bart's Reading Room." He paused for effect. Landon could scarcely breathe. "What did you do, go out for a bite to eat? You must have been starved, especially since you hardly touched your pancakes this morning." This was directed at Landon.

"Well," Landon said as his stomach involuntarily growled, "we did snack on some oranges." This was certainly true. No lying here.

"And bread," said Holly.

"And ginger ale," added Bridget, jiggling the Coke.

"Humph." Their mother's expression softened. "That's not much for lunch. You need to eat more than bread and oranges. What café down there serves—"

"Uh, Grandpa?" said Landon. He tried to step from his mother's gaze, but he felt her eyes still on him. "What kind of seafood are we having?"

Was it Landon's imagination, or had Grandpa Karl's eyes actually glimmered with a sealike shine? In any case, after he responded, "Stuffed crab legs," he gave his grandchildren a sly wink.

Epilogue

Winterwild had a football rematch against their rival Tangleriver later in the season. Winterwild had, in fact, lost that first game, when Landon saw the animals and was pulled. Not the rematch, however. With his mom and dad and sisters cheering him on, Landon scored two running touchdowns, one of which was right up the middle for forty yards. This time, Jake Adams wasn't quick enough to catch the determined Landon Snow. And Landon made it through the entire game without seeing any animals or hearing any strange chants.

When the school year ended, Landon, Holly, and Bridget were looking forward to an extended stay with their grandparents in Button Up, while their mom and dad went on an Alaska cruise.

"Sorry about not taking you with us," their parents apologized. "We do promise to take a family trip to the ocean someday."

Landon wondered if his sisters had as hard a time as he did keeping a straight face. He tried to look disappointed when, in fact, he was both remembering the incredible sea adventure he and Holly and Bridget had already experienced, as well as anticipating their next journey to the Button Up Library. *And we'll be with Grandma and Grandpa for a whole week this time,* thought Landon excitedly, *not just a long weekend.*

Later that same night, Landon lay half asleep in his bed when a high-pitched scream jolted him awake. A blue light was blinking outside, causing his shade to faintly pulse.

What on earth?

Landon crept to his bedroom window and peeked from behind the curtain. Across the street, a squad car door opened and a policeman stepped out. He had stopped another vehicle for something.

Landon's breath steamed the window, and he stepped back. Nighttime in Minnesota could be cool even during the summer. Red lights were twirling, as well, intermittently with the blue. But the red seemed to only slide by, while the blue lit Landon's window like a high-speed lighthouse beam.

Landon waited until the scene was over and the two cars had driven off. It was probably just a speeding ticket or something. The flashing blue light, along with the whine of the siren—for that's what he had heard, not a scream—stirred up another image he hadn't thought about in months. In fact, he had nearly forgotten it.

He was inside the entrance to the animal keep on the Island of Arcanum when there had been an ear-piercing shriek along with a burst of blue light. Landon also recalled Dot laying out little animal bones in the shape of five animals: a bird, a fish, a lizard, a snake, and a bat. At that point, Griggs had asked, *What sort of arcane alchemy are they up to, anyway?*

Landon realized he had never looked up those words.

Flipping on his desk lamp, Landon removed the dictionary from the shelf. *"Arcane,"* he muttered. It was *Arcan* with an *e* at the end. *That can't be good.* He shuddered at the thought of those tall creatures with the black unseeing eyes. Ah, here it was.

"Secret or mysterious," he said softly, "as in the secret practices of a cult." No, this didn't sound good at all.

With slightly trembling fingers—*I'm just tired,* Landon thought, *that's all*—he turned back to *alchemy.*

The first definition had to do with the combination of a medieval science and philosophy aimed at, among other things, changing base metals into gold.

Landon glanced up. "The coin," he whispered. Had the great gold coin that had been tossed from the Echoing Green been a result of alchemy? He shrugged to himself. Perhaps he would never know. The next definition at first didn't strike him as peculiar one way or another. As he thought about it, however, picturing a bird, a bat, a snake, a fish, and a lizard—*and possibly other animals or things, those were only the bones Dot gathered*—being mixed somehow into an Arcan fire, well, what could this second definition possibly mean?

"Alchemy: a force or ability of changing usual, ordinary things into the unusual or extraordinary."

Landon's throat felt dry. He closed the dictionary and put it back on the shelf. He was about to go get a glass of water—it would be good to step out of his room for a moment and then come back to find everything normal again—when another book began to move.

This had never happened before—not here, not in his room. Landon froze, watching first from the corner of his eye before gradually turning to face his Bible—Bartholomew G. Benneford's ancient Bible—which had been lying open on his bedside stand. When the last page floated down, Landon waited a moment before approaching. It was open to the final book, the book of Revelation, to a page with these underlined words in chapter twelve:

> *And there was war in heaven: Michael and his angels fought against the dragon; and the dragon fought and his angels, and prevailed not; neither was their place found any more in heaven. And the great dragon was cast out, that old serpent, called the Devil, and Satan, which deceiveth the whole world: he was cast out into the earth, and his angels were cast out with him.*

Landon's heart hammered as things began to come together in his mind. This was too incredible, too unreal. Yet there it was in the Bible.

The pages began to turn again, fluttering from left to right before settling in the book of Ephesians. Underlined were these words in chapter six:

> *Put on the whole armour of God, that ye may be able to stand against the wiles of the devil. For we wrestle not against flesh and blood, but against principalities, against powers, against the rulers of the darkness of this world, against spiritual wickedness in high places.*

Landon took a deep breath and closed his eyes. No matter what sort of arcane—*or Arcan*—alchemy he might face, there was nothing in this world or any other that could harm someone protected by the Auctor's armor.

Was there?

Landon went to the kitchen and filled a glass with water. After drinking it, he returned to bed, feeling better. Soon he was fast asleep, dreaming of another trip to the Button Up Library.

About the Author

R. K. Mortenson, an ordained minister in the Church of the Lutheran Brethren, has been writing poems and stories since he was a kid. *Landon Snow and the Island of Arcanum* is his third novel. Mortenson currently serves as a navy chaplain in Florida. He lives with his wife, daughter, and son in Jacksonville.

Other books by R. K. Mortenson:

Landon Snow
and the Auctor's Riddle

Landon Snow
and the Shadows of Malus Quidam

Be Sure to Watch for:

Landon Snow

and the Igneus Forest

Coming Spring 2007!